The Best Christmas Present Ever

The Best Christmas Present Ever

SYLVIA GREEN

■SCHOLASTIC

For Charles and Layla-May

Scholastic Children's Books
A division of Scholastic Ltd
Euston House, 24 Eversholt Street
London, NW1 1DB, UK
Registered office: Westfield Road, Southam, Warwickshire, CV47 0RA
SCHOLASTIC and associated logos are trademarks and/or registered trademarks of Scholastic Inc.

The Best Dog in the World
First published in the UK by Scholastic Ltd, 2005
Text copyright © Sylvia Green, 2005
Illustrations copyright © Sophie Keen, 2005

The Best Christmas Ever
First published in the UK by Scholastic Ltd, 2000
Text copyright © Sylvia Green, 2000
Illustrations copyright © Chris Chapman, 2000

The Christmas Pony
First published in the UK by Scholastic Ltd, 2001
Text copyright © Sylvia Green, 2001
Illustrations copyright © Sharon Scotland, 2001

This edition published in the UK by Scholastic Ltd, 2011

Cover illustration © Sophy Williams, 2011

The moral rights of the author and illustrators of this work have been asserted by them.

ISBN 978 1 407 12936 5

A CIP catalogue record for this book is available from the British Library.

Printed by CPI Mackays, Chatham, ME5 8TD
Papers used by Scholastic Children's Books are made from wood grown in sustainable forests.

1 3 5 7 9 10 8 6 4 2

www.scholastic.co.uk/zone

The Best Dog
in the World

Chapter 1

Elliot
The Dogs' Home

Elliot turned the corner and there was the dogs' home. He quickened his pace. "I don't know why I didn't think of this months ago," he said to himself. "As soon as Mum ruined all my hopes of having a pet. Why on earth did she have to go and marry boring old Myles?"

He felt a bit guilty as soon as he'd said it. Myles was always nice to him.

"But he is boring and she knew I wanted her to marry someone with a nice house and garden in the country," said Elliot.

"Somewhere where I could keep lots of animals."

Myles not only didn't have a house and a garden in the country, he didn't have a house at all. He'd moved into their small flat with them! Their small flat where they weren't allowed to keep any pets.

And the absolute worst thing of all was that Myles was allergic to animals. Anything with fur or feathers made him start sneezing and brought him out in a rash.

Elliot reached the gate and smiled as an assortment of barks greeted him. He instantly pictured the different dogs, the big ones with the deep throaty woofs right down to the small ones with high pitched yaps. He couldn't wait to see them.

There was a bell on the wall with a sign

that read: Please ring and Nick or Angela will be with you shortly.

Elliot eagerly pressed the bell.

A tall man appeared straight away. "Hello there," he said. "What can I do for you?"

Elliot guessed it was Nick. "Hi, I'm Elliot. I've come to help you with the dogs."

Nick smiled at him. "Well, Elliot, that's very kind of you, but I'm afraid children aren't allowed to help with the dogs."

Elliot's face fell.

"But I really love animals – especially dogs – and I just want to spend some time with them. I live close by and I don't mind what I do."

"Maybe your mum or your dad could adopt you a dog from here," suggested Nick. "There are lots that need a good home and—"

"They can't," Elliot interrupted him. "I haven't got a real dad – just Mum – and Myles." Then he told him about Myles and his allergy and the flats where they lived.

Nick looked sorry for him. "Look, I can spare ten minutes, how about if I take you to meet one or two of the dogs? At least you can have a chat with them."

Elliot brightened up. "Perhaps I can cheer them up a bit."

"Sure," said Nick, opening the gate. "We do our best for them but we're always so busy, we don't get time to give them as much individual attention as we'd like."

As Elliot followed Nick over to the runs, all the dogs started barking and jumping up at the wire. "They do this every time someone comes in," said Nick. "They're hoping you've come to adopt them."

He introduced him to Sam, a lively Labrador, whose elderly owner could no longer cope with him. Then to Flash, a greyhound that had been retired from racing. Opposite them was Bella, a sleek black poodle who had one blue eye and one yellow eye.

"Bella's owners bred her for a show dog," Nick explained. "But with two different coloured eyes she wouldn't win any prizes so they didn't want to keep her."

"That's awful," said Elliot. "Fancy getting rid of her because of that."

"At least they brought her in here and didn't just dump her, the way some people do," said Nick. "And I'm afraid we also get animals that have been ill-treated or neglected. There are some strange people around."

Elliot wanted a dog so badly, he found it hard to believe people could be like that.

"And this –" said Nick, pointing to a bundle of matted, brown fur lying in the next run – "is Denzil. He's a stray – been living rough for some time by the looks of him. The dog warden picked him up hanging round the back of McDonald's."

Elliot peered into the run. It looked just like a heap of dog hair that someone had swept up but then he saw it was moving gently as the animal breathed. He stared at the tangled mass and could just pick out a long shaggy ear and then a longer furry mass at the other end that had to be his tail.

Then he noticed his feet – big, hairy, ungainly feet. Denzil was the scruffiest dog he'd ever seen.

Chapter 2

Denzil
King of the Road

Denzil was dreaming of hamburgers. He could hear all the other dogs barking. They were obviously jealous of his HUGE hamburger. He could almost taste it. . .

"Hello, Denzil."

The voice interrupted his dream – just as he was about to take a bite. He opened one eye and peered through his tangled mass of hair. A boy was standing there looking at him.

"Hey, you're a great dog," said the boy.

Great? thought Denzil. *Me?* No one

had ever said that to him. It was usually a case of "Look at the state of that one" before they moved on to look at the other dogs – the ones that actually wanted to be adopted. The ones that were jumping up at the wire and barking right now. *Some dogs*, thought Denzil, *just have no pride.*

Denzil couldn't understand a dog wanting to be owned by anyone. A free spirit, that was him. King of the road – his own boss. He went where he liked, when he liked. *All right, so I've been picked up at the moment,* he admitted to himself. *But I'll be on my way again very soon.*

"I'm Elliot," said the boy.

Denzil opened his other eye. *Why's he telling me his name? I hope he doesn't expect me to shake paws or anything.* Denzil wasn't into doing tricks for humans.

"Can I stroke him?" asked Elliot.

The boy was with Nick. Nick was OK, and so was his wife, Angela. They treated him pretty well and the food was quite good here too.

Denzil was an expert on dogs' homes; he'd been picked up and put in several over the years. But he always managed to escape – after he'd had a few good meals.

"OK, you can stroke him," said Nick, unbolting the door. "He's actually very docile, for a stray."

Docile? thought Denzil. *Of course I'm docile. Just because I'm a dog of the road* (he hated the word stray) *doesn't mean I'm going to savage everyone!* His mother had been a dog of the road too and she'd been very proud of the fact. She'd taught Denzil a lot about life, and he'd gone on to learn more himself over the years. Denzil was a pretty streetwise dog by now. He knew what was what.

Nick brought the boy into his run. He kept perfectly still as Elliot bent down and gently stroked him on his head and over his long shaggy ears. Only his eyes moved as he watched for any sudden movement. He didn't trust humans.

Elliot stroked him all the way down his back to the long tangled mass that was his tail. "He's such a great dog," he said.

Nick chuckled. "Why do you like this one so much?"

"I don't know," said Elliot. "He's different – kind of special." *Special?* Denzil had been called a lot of things in his life, but never special.

Then Elliot picked up an old rubber

ball that was lying next to him. "Come on, Denzil," he said, rolling it across the run. "Fetch it, boy. Fetch the ball."

You kidding? thought Denzil. *I don't do "fetch". Why should I? I don't want the ball – and if he wants it, he can fetch it himself.*

"I don't think he's used to playing," said Nick. "And I'm sorry, but I've got to get back to work so you'll have to go home now."

Elliot looked disappointed. "OK. But can I come and see him again?"

Nick chuckled. "All right. As long as Angela or myself are around."

Denzil watched Nick bolt the door behind them. *Why does Elliot want to see me again?* he wondered.

As soon as they'd gone, Bella, the poodle in the next run came over to the wire. "So you've finally clicked then," she snapped. "Course, the poor boy must be short-sighted. Must have forgotten his glasses."

"What are you talking about?" asked Denzil, sitting up for a good scratch.

"Don't listen to her," said Flash, the greyhound. "She's just jealous that the boy wants to adopt you and not her."

"Adopt me?" Denzil jumped to his feet. "I don't want to be adopted. Not by anyone."

"Why not?" asked Sam, the Labrador. "Every dog wants a nice comfortable home with kind people to look after them."

"Not me," said Denzil. "I'll be escaping from here – and soon. I've got places to go, new smells to sniff. I'm a free spirit." He'd heard about living with humans – there were responsibilities attached. You had to chew slippers and chase the postman. And for some reason they kept throwing things like balls and sticks and then expecting you to fetch them back.

He gave himself a good shake and bits of fur flew everywhere.

"Ugh, you're disgusting," said Bella, jumping back, her blue and yellow eyes flashing. "The sooner I get adopted the better. I'm bound to get a really good home, my previous owners were heartbroken when they had to give me up."

Denzil didn't answer her. If that was what she wanted to believe, that was up to her. But he'd seen it all before – dogs bought or bred as show dogs, then if there was something even slightly wrong with them, they were got rid of.

That was humans for you.

Then there was Flash. He'd been a really good racing greyhound, won lots of races for his owner. But now he was too old to race. . .

"What sort of dog are you anyway?" asked Bella.

"Me? I'm a Bitsa," said Denzil.

"I've never heard of a Bitsa," said Sam.

"It means I'm bitsa this breed and bitsa that breed," said Denzil. "I've got a bit of Irish Wolfhound in me, a bit of Old English Sheepdog, some Labrador, bloodhound. . ." He paused and looked at Bella. "I don't think I've got any poodle."

Bella looked at him haughtily. "Definitely not," she said.

They were interrupted by Angela opening Denzil's run. "Come on, Denzil, let's give you a bath to spruce you up a bit."

Denzil sighed. It was the same, every time he got picked up — they always wanted to give him a bath. But the truth of the matter was, he never looked any different!

Chapter 3

Elliot

If only. . .

Elliot went back to the dogs' home the very next day. He met Abbie and Kai McFarlane, who were in his class at school, just coming out with their father. He felt a pang of jealously as he saw they had Sam the Labrador on a lead.

"Hi, Elliot," said Abbie. "We've just adopted Sam."

"Isn't he great?" said Kai. "Have you come to adopt a dog too?"

"No." Elliot stooped to make a fuss of Sam. "I'm not allowed to."

He watched them leave, Sam's tail wagging enthusiastically. Then Nick told him that Angela was cleaning out the runs, so he could go and chat to Denzil while she was there.

Elliot went straight over. Angela had finished cleaning Denzil's run and was just letting him out of his kennel. The dog ambled out into his run and looked up at Elliot. Elliot thought he looked a bit surprised.

"Hi, Denzil. I bet you didn't expect to see me again so soon, did you?"

Angela smiled at Elliot. "Come to keep Denzil company, have you? Nick told me how much you like him."

Elliot nodded.

"I gave him a bath yesterday," said Angela, as she started hosing down Bella's run. "But he doesn't look any different."

Elliot smiled at the scruffy dog. "He looks great, just as he is."

He intended to visit Denzil as often as he could – as long as he was there – as long as someone hadn't adopted him, or. . .

"What happens to dogs that no one adopts?" he asked Angela.

"Well, we try to re-home them for as long as possible," she told him. "We don't like to give up, but space is limited especially now, just after Christmas. It's a very busy time of year. Some people buy dogs for Christmas presents then either the puppy grows bigger than they expected or they just get fed up with looking after them."

"That's awful," said Elliot. "I'd never get fed up, or worry about how big they got – if I had a dog."

Angela smiled at him. "Puppies are quite easy to find new homes for, but not all dogs are suitable for re-homing. You get the odd vicious one and then there's the strays. Long-term strays are not usually house-trained – which tends to put people off – and they don't always bond with humans."

"Is Denzil what you'd call a long-term stray?" asked Elliot.

"Well, yes, he is," said Angela. "But like I said, we don't like to give up."

"But what if you do have to give up?" Elliot persisted. He felt he just had to know.

"Well, only if we're full up and we need the space," Angela began slowly. "And only if they've been here a long time and we really don't think there's any hope of them being adopted. Well, we have to take them to the vet. . ."

19

She didn't finish. She didn't have to. Elliot shut his eyes to keep out the dreadful image. That wasn't going to happen to Denzil – it just couldn't.

"Hey, cheer up," said Angela. "There are lots of really kind people around. Maybe someone will want to take Denzil on."

Elliot smiled at her. Then he turned back to Denzil and took a red ball out of his pocket. "Here, Denzil, I've brought you a new ball as you didn't seem to like the one you've got." Denzil really seemed to be listening to him this time. He was watching him with his beautiful black eyes – at least, what Elliot could see of them through the dog's tangled hair. "It's really my ball," Elliot told him. "But you can have it."

He tossed it over the wire into the run but Denzil ignored it as it bounced around him. "Oh well, I expect you'll play with it later when I've gone," said Elliot.

He stayed talking to Denzil until Angela had finished cleaning the runs.

Elliot walked home deep in thought. Someone would be bound to adopt Denzil – but then he'd never see him again. And the alternative didn't bear thinking about. He knew it would only be a last resort because Nick and Angela really cared about the dogs.

If only there was a way he could adopt Denzil.

The lift was broken again so he climbed the eighty-eight steps up to their flat. He wanted to talk to Mum about Denzil but she was resting. She'd just given up her job as a nurse because she was expecting a baby soon – hers and Myles's baby. A sudden image of a frilly baby's bonnet flashed into Elliot's mind. Peeping out of the bonnet was a tiny Myles face complete with glasses.

Myles was putting up a shelf, for yet more of his books. He had loads of them and he even worked in a bookshop. He spent loads of time reading and never played any sports or anything. Elliot supposed it was something to do with him being old – he was almost forty! Several years older than Elliot's mum.

On the table was a book on bringing up babies and another one on babies' names. A third book was open at the page showing how to put up a shelf.

Myles was really enthusiastic about his shelf. "Tell you what, Elliot. You can help me, if you like," he said.

Elliot sighed and passed him the screwdriver but his mind wasn't on the job. It was back at the dogs' home with Denzil. He was going to visit him as often as he could – as long as he was still there – and he was going take him lots of treats.

Chapter 4

Denzil
"They're not getting a lead on me!"

A week later Denzil was still at the home. He'd never stayed in one so long. He slumped down on the floor of his run – but immediately jumped up again as a high-pitched squeak came from under him.

He looked down crossly at the stupid bone-shaped bit of rubber. *Why on earth would Elliot think I wanted an imitation bone that squeaks?* he wondered for probably the fiftieth time. Then he looked at the rubber chicken, the large stick and the bright red ball. Elliot kept bringing him things, and he'd been back every day the past week.

"So why haven't you escaped yet?" Bella interrupted his thoughts. "What's keeping you?" The proud black poodle was in a bad mood. She'd really thought a couple were going to adopt her that morning and then, at the last moment, they'd chosen a little brown and white spaniel instead. She was sure it was just because both the spaniel's eyes were the same colour, unlike hers.

"I'll be back on the road any day now," said Denzil.

"It's that boy, isn't it?" snapped Bella. "All your talk about being a 'dog of the road' and not wanting to be adopted. You're no different to the rest of us."

Denzil shook himself irritably. "I've told you, I don't want to be adopted," he barked.

"I'll go when it suits me – it's nothing to do with the boy."

"He has been back several times," Flash pointed out. "And he never looks at any of the other dogs – it's just you he's interested in."

"He stays for ages," said Bella. "And brings you presents."

"What do I want presents for?" Denzil turned tail on her and went to lie down at the back of his run. The truth was, he didn't really know himself why he hadn't escaped yet. He only usually stayed in a rescue home long enough to have a couple of good meals and then he was off. Back on the open road where he belonged. There'd never been a home he couldn't escape from yet and he'd already worked out how to slide the bolt on this door by watching Nick and Angela.

So why was he still here? Denzil didn't really understand it himself, he was usually itching to get away. It couldn't be anything to do with Elliot – he didn't need anyone. The nearest Denzil had ever got to having a friend was Harvey, the soft-hearted sheepdog, who he'd met in one of the homes. Harvey now lived on a turkey farm and Denzil visited him sometimes. He'd been invited to stay but he'd never even been tempted.

Denzil made a decision. He'd go tomorrow, after breakfast, and then maybe he'd find the remains of a hamburger for dinner. He licked his lips. He hadn't had a good hamburger for ages.

"Hey, Denzil. I'm back." It was Elliot. Denzil found himself getting up to greet him. Well, it was the least he could do as he was leaving tomorrow.

"Look what I've brought you today," said Elliot, holding out a bag. "Super Whopper Doggy Chocs."

Super what? thought Denzil. *What on earth am I supposed to do with them?*

Elliot opened the bag and took out a couple of large, round, brown shapes. He pushed them through the wire. "I bought them with my pocket money."

Denzil sniffed them. They smelt nice. He'd smelt something similar once before when a little girl had dropped something she was eating in the park. Her mother hadn't let her pick it up again but Denzil had been happy to pick it up – and eat it!

Denzil quickly ate up all the Super Whopper Doggy Chocs. This was the kind of present he liked.

"Guess what?" said Elliot. "Nick says I can take you for a walk today. He's going to give Flash some exercise so he says I can go with him and take you as well."

A *walk?* thought Denzil. *Oh no, that's going too far. I don't need anyone to take me for a walk.*

"I've got a lead for you here," said Elliot, whipping it out of his pocket. "Nick's going to put it on you for me."

Oh no, he's not, thought Denzil. *I'm king of the open road – a free spirit. They're not getting a lead on me.*

Nick arrived and slid the bolt on the door and he and Elliot came into the run. Denzil shrank back against the wall of his kennel.

"Oh come on, Denzil," said Elliot, bending down to him. "It'll be fun."

Denzil looked up at him. Elliot had brought him Super Whopper Doggy Chocs and he had said he was a great dog. No one had ever said that about him before. A mangy mutt, he'd been called only recently when he was helping himself to a burnt sausage out of a man's dustbin. Why the man had been so protective about a burnt sausage he couldn't imagine. He'd obviously thrown it away in the first place! Denzil would never understand humans.

"Please, Denzil," said Elliot.

Denzil looked into his eyes. There was something there – a sadness – but a kind of longing too. He slowly came forward. *I suppose it won't do any harm,* he thought. *And it is for Elliot's sake – the boy has been kind to me.*

He allowed Nick to put the collar and

lead on him. He didn't like the collar, it was uncomfortable and felt itchy. He only ever wore one when he'd been picked up by the dog warden.

Nick gave the lead to Elliot and went to get Flash, then the four of them walked towards the big field. Denzil pretended to let Elliot lead him and padded along beside him on his over-large paws. He knew he was walking on his own but if Elliot wanted to think he was leading him, then it was OK.

Wait a minute, he thought. *What am I doing? I've never wanted to please a human before.*

Chapter 5

Elliot
"I wish you really were my dog."

Elliot happily led Denzil round the field. He'd met Abbie and Kai, walking Sam, on his way to the home. Now it was his turn. He was pretending that Denzil really was his dog and he was just taking him for his daily walk.

Nick was being pulled ahead by Flash, who was obviously used to going a lot faster.

Elliot decided to run too. "Come on, boy," he called to Denzil, tugging gently at his lead.

Denzil resisted a bit at first but then he began to run alongside Elliot. After a while he started to bound ahead and Elliot had to run faster to keep up with him. Round and round the field they went, the dog's large paws pounding the ground and his long shaggy ears bouncing up and down. They overtook Nick and Flash not just once, but twice.

Elliot laughed out loud as the wind blew in his hair. "Wow, you can really go, Denzil," he called. "Oh, this is just great!"

All too soon it was time for Denzil to go back in his run. Elliot was quite out of breath and his face was glowing in the cold air as he said goodbye.

He ruffled Denzil's shaggy coat. "Oh, Denzil, I wish, I wish, I wish that you really were my dog. I wish, I really wish that I could take you home with me."

Denzil stared up at him, panting, his long tongue hanging out. His tangled hair was swept back from his face and Elliot thought that his black eyes looked puzzled. "Don't worry, Denzil, I'll be back soon," Elliot told him. "You're just the best dog in the whole world."

Elliot was thoughtful as he walked home. Every time he went to the home he was relieved to find Denzil was still there. He was pleased no one had adopted him, although he couldn't understand why – even though he was a long-term stray. He was easily the best dog there.

But several more dogs had been taken into the home that week and it was actually full. In fact Sam's old run now had two smaller dogs in it. They were running short of space and Denzil couldn't stay there for ever. . .

"Nick and Angela know how much I love him," he reassured himself. "Surely they won't let anything happen. . . Oh, if only I could find a way to keep him myself."

Mum was waiting for him when he arrived home. "Myles has got a surprise for you," she told him. "He's in your room."

Elliot quickly went into his bedroom. Myles was in there putting up a shelf. He gave Elliot a beaming smile.

"This is for your books," he told him. "And in particular, your book – on goldfish."

"But, I haven't got. . ." Elliot started.

Then he saw the book with a large orange goldfish on the cover lying on his bed. "OK, I have got a book on goldfish," he said. "You've bought me one. But why?"

He stopped as his eyes followed to where Myles was pointing. On his chest of drawers was a bowl with two goldfish in. They had a little bridge to swim under and some dark green water weed planted in the multi-coloured gravel at the bottom.

"I know how much you want a pet," said Myles. "And I'm not allergic to fish, so I bought them for you."

"Well – er – thanks," said Elliot. "But we're not allowed to keep *any* pets in the flats."

"Oh, I don't think anyone will complain about a couple of fish," he said. "After all they're not going to make much noise, are they?" Myles laughed and then Mum came in and laughed too. She always thought Myles's jokes were hilarious.

"Wasn't it kind of Myles?" she said.

"Yes, it was," said Elliot. And it was kind of him – it was just that. . . Then Elliot spotted the cot folded up behind the door. "Why's that in here?"

"Well, the baby will be sharing your room," said Mum. "We've only got two bedrooms and you've got plenty of space in here."

"I'm going to fix it up really nice for the two of you," said Myles. "It'll be fun for you to have someone to share with – apart from the fish, of course." He laughed again and Mum joined in.

Elliot had a quick vision of the baby in the frilly bonnet that looked just like Myles again. Only this time it was sitting on the shelf in his room reading a book!

He watched the illegal fish swimming round in their bowl. They were nice, but he didn't want to share his room with the new baby. He wouldn't mind sharing it with Denzil though.

Chapter 6

Denzil
A Ginormous Decision

Denzil was worried. Two days had now passed since he'd decided to escape from the home – but he was still there.

What's up with me? he thought. *It's not that I can't escape.* He'd even got as far as sliding the bolt on the door last night but somehow he couldn't bring himself to actually go.

He kept thinking about when Elliot was coming again.

At least Bella had stopped getting at him – a little girl and her mum had decided to adopt her. The little girl thought that Bella's different coloured eyes were "really sweet" and they were picking her up that afternoon. That was one happy poodle.

Flash had been taken to somewhere called Greyhound Rescue where he could live happily with other greyhounds. Several other dogs had been re-homed but more had come in. A couple of times he'd caught Nick looking at him and saying to Angela, "I don't know what we're going to do about Denzil." Well, they didn't have to do anything about him – he was his own boss – a free spirit. He'd sort himself out, as he always had.

Denzil lay down in his run and put his paws over his ears to shut out the noise of the other dogs barking. "I must be mad staying here. Especially as Elliot only comes for a little while each day." He sat straight up again. He'd finally admitted it. He was staying just so he could see Elliot. It was quite a shock to him.

Elliot arrived in the afternoon. Denzil immediately jumped up and wagged his shaggy tail in greeting.

"I bet you thought I wasn't coming, didn't you?" said Elliot. "Well, Myles decided to cook the lunch, as it's Saturday. He's bought this cook book on healthy eating and he decided to make his own hamburgers. It took ages."

Denzil's ears pricked up. They had hamburgers at their house!

Nick came and put Denzil's lead on and Elliot was allowed to walk him round the field on his own. They walked and ran together and jumped over logs and all the time Elliot talked to him and laughed.

Denzil was baffled. *Why is this so much fun?* he wondered. He'd never been one for running about unless it was necessary – like when he was being chased off by someone. *But it is fun,* he thought. He'd never felt so happy. *It must be – it can only be – Elliot.*

It was after Nick had put him back in his run and Elliot was saying goodbye that Denzil made his decision. A ginormous, momentous, decision. He wanted to be with Elliot – always. He even wanted Elliot to take him home with him. (And it wasn't just because they had hamburgers at their house.) He actually wanted to be adopted!

I can't believe it, he thought. *Me, Denzil, king of the road, free spirit, I want to be adopted – by Elliot.*

All he had to do was let him know. *Elliot's always saying he wishes he could take me home with him,* he thought. *Well now he can.*

Denzil knew what to do. He'd seen the other dogs do it often enough. He started jumping up at the wire and barking. He felt a bit self-conscious at first but he had to let Elliot know that he wanted him to adopt him.

Elliot laughed. "It's all right, Denzil, I'll be back tomorrow."

He wasn't getting the message.

I'll have to try the soulful eyes, thought Denzil. *That never fails. Gets 'em every time.*

Denzil had never lowered himself to anything like this before but he managed the most beautiful soulful eyes as he looked pleadingly up at Elliot.

That certainly moved him. Elliot had

tears in his eyes as he crouched down to speak to him.

"Hey, Denzil. You're the greatest dog in the world, you know that? And I really wish I could take you home with me, but I'm not allowed."

Then he was gone, leaving Denzil completely baffled.

The little girl and the lady arrived to collect Bella. The poodle paused as she was led past Denzil. There was concern in her blue and yellow eyes. "I'm sorry, Denzil. I really thought he wanted to adopt you. You'll find someone else, you'll see."

But Denzil didn't see. He didn't just want to be adopted – he wanted to be with Elliot. Why wasn't he allowed to take him?

"I've got it," he said. "He's not allowed to adopt me because he's too small. Whenever someone comes to collect a dog – like that little girl who's just taken Bella – they have a big person with them. Grown-ups, they're called."

The more he thought about it, the more sure he was. Elliot always came on his own. Maybe his grown-up couldn't come. Or maybe he didn't have one. Poor Elliot.

There was only one thing for it – he'd have to take matters into his own paws.

Denzil jumped up and, pushing his nose up against the wire, managed to grasp the bolt with his teeth. A quick, expert flick of his head and the door swung open.

Then he was off, wind blowing through his fur as he raced after Elliot, following his scent. *Good job I've got a bit of bloodhound in me,* he thought.

Chapter 7

Elliot
"What am I going to do with you?"

Elliot turned round in surprise as he heard a bark. The next minute he was hit by a flurry of tangled fur jumping up at him.

"Denzil! What, are you doing here?" He knew Nick had bolted the door, he'd seen him do it. "How did you get out?"

A long pink tongue started licking his face.

Elliot laughed and wiped his wet face with his sleeve. "It's great that you're so pleased to see me but you can't stay out here – I'll have to take you back."

Denzil immediately jumped away from him and barked.

"What's the matter, boy? Don't you like the home?"

Denzil barked again and backed away.

"I suppose you can't want to be in the home or you wouldn't have escaped," said Elliot. "But what am I going to do with you?"

Denzil crept forward again. "I can't just leave you loose – you might get injured. Plus you might get lost and then I'll never see you again."

Denzil looked up at him, his head cocked to one side. He looked puzzled.

Elliot ruffled his fur. "And I can't take you home with me."

He looked into the dog's eyes and could see he was hurt, very hurt. Elliot couldn't bear it. Denzil had obviously escaped to be with him. What was he going to do?

"I know." He had a sudden idea. "I could take you to Abbie and Kai's. They adopted Sam, remember? They love dogs and I'm sure one more won't make any difference – and I'll even be able to come and visit you there."

Denzil still looked puzzled but he trotted alongside Elliot as he walked to the twins' house.

Sam's barking greeted them from the other side of the door when Elliot knocked.

The twins' mother opened it holding on to Sam's collar.

"Hello, Mrs McFarlane," Elliot started.

But she wasn't looking at him – she was looking at Denzil. "What's that?" she exclaimed.

"It's a dog," Elliot told her indignantly. "He's called Denzil."

"It looks more like a filthy old floor mop with legs," said Mrs McFarlane.

Elliot bent down and covered Denzil's ears. "Please don't say that, you'll hurt his feelings. He needs a home – at least, for now."

"Well he's not coming in my house," said Mrs McFarlane, struggling to hold Sam back. "This one is quite enough to look after." She closed the door.

It opened again immediately and Abbie and Kai were there. Sam shot out to greet Denzil and the two dogs happily went off to investigate the front garden.

"We heard what happened," said Kai.

"I suppose you're not allowed to keep animals in your flats," said Abbie.

"No," said Elliot. "Although Mrs Phipps

has a secret cat which only goes out on her balcony and Mr Barns has a budgie. And now I've got two goldfish, but it's not just that." He told her about Myles and his allergy.

"Our dad says he's allergic to grass seed," said Abbie. "But Mum says it's all in his mind – he just doesn't want to do the gardening."

Elliot was thoughtful. "D'you think it can be just in the mind? D'you think maybe Myles isn't really allergic to animals – he just thinks he is?"

"Could be," said Abbie. "Have you ever seen him with an animal?"

"No I haven't, he just said that he comes out in a rash and starts sneezing every time he gets near anything with fur or feathers."

"Well, you could always test him out," said Kai. "Get Denzil near to him without him knowing."

"I could, couldn't I?" said Elliot.

He remembered that Mum and Myles were going shopping for a pram and other baby things that afternoon so they'd probably still be out. All he had to do was smuggle Denzil into his room. He'd have to keep him hidden, with animals not being allowed in the flats. But with Mrs Phipps's secret cat, Mr Barns's budgie and his illegal goldfish, what difference would one more creature make?

He made the decision.

"Come on, Denzil," he called. "I'm taking you home."

Denzil happily bounded alongside him as they raced over to Elliot's flats.

Amazingly, no one seemed to be around. Denzil was a bit reluctant to go inside the building but Elliot eventually persuaded him to climb the stairs. (He knew he wouldn't like the lift, even though it was working now.) Elliot opened the door to his flat and led Denzil into the living room.

"I'll have to keep you hidden in my room for now," he told him. "I'll sneak you out for a walk later when they're watching TV. Then tomorrow I'll let you out and Myles will be so surprised that you've been here all evening and night. I bet he'll be really pleased to find he isn't allergic after all."

Denzil immediately started sniffing round the furniture. Elliot smiled as he watched him.

"D'you like it here, Denzil?" Then the

scruffy dog sat down on the carpet and had a good scratch.

"No, come on, boy, you've got to go in my room."

Denzil stood up and shook himself, fur was flying everywhere. "Oh no," cried Elliot. "I'll have to get this all cleared up before they get back."

He managed to get Denzil into his room and had just shut the door behind him when Mum and Myles came in.

Elliot watched in horror as wisps of fur wafted across the room towards them.

Myles sniffed a couple of times then he started sneezing. His eyes streamed and his face rapidly turned all red and blotchy.

Chapter 8

Denzil

"He's not even house-trained!"

Denzil was startled by all the noise coming from the other room. And in any case he was beginning to feel claustrophobic – he'd never been inside a house before and he hated being shut in.

He barked and jumped up at the door. It flew open and he bounded out.

A lady with a big tummy screamed and a strange man with a red blotchy face was sneezing all over the place. Elliot was crying and saying he was sorry. Whatever could he have done?

Elliot wouldn't have done anything wrong, so Denzil started barking again to tell them.

"For goodness sake, get him out of here," shouted the lady with the big tummy. "I'll have to thoroughly clean the whole flat now."

It looked all right to Denzil.

"And look," she screamed, pointing to the bedroom doorway. "He's not even house-trained!" Denzil saw Elliot's mouth drop open as he looked at the offending pile on the bedroom carpet.

What's wrong with that? thought Denzil. *Doesn't everyone do it?*

Elliot wiped his eyes on his sleeve and bent down to Denzil gently tugging at the tangled fur on the back of his neck. "Come on, boy."

He led him past the sneezing man whose face had turned almost purple now, right to the tips of his ears.

"And come straight back," called the lady, as they went out of the door.

Make your mind up, thought Denzil. *You just told him to go.*

Humans were always strange but those two seemed stranger than usual. Elliot led him down the stairs. He was different, he was OK and Denzil was happy just to be with him. *I wonder where we're going next?* he thought.

Out in the street, it had started to snow. Elliot bent down to Denzil. "I'm really sorry," he told him. "But I can't think of anywhere else you can go. I'll have to take you back to the home."

Denzil immediately pulled away from

him. He looked up at Elliot. *Did he say, take me back to the home?*

"Oh, come on, Denzil," Elliot pleaded. "I can't just leave you wandering round the streets. You'll have to go back."

Oh no I won't. Denzil turned tail on him and ran. He ran till he was sure Elliot had stopped following him, then he slowed down to a trot.

A large tabby cat came round the corner. "Hey, Denzil," said the cat. "Haven't seen you around for a while."

"I've been away," Denzil growled softly. "But I'm back now – for good."

As the cat went on its way, Denzil spotted a hamburger carton lying in the gutter. But he didn't even bother to investigate it, he'd completely lost his appetite. He flopped down behind an old building.

He'd never felt so hurt. This was the first time in his whole life that he'd trusted anyone. The first time he'd decided that he wanted to be with someone and he – Elliot – didn't want him. It was just as he'd always thought, humans weren't to be trusted – not any of them – not even Elliot!

Denzil lay down with his head on his paws, snowflakes gently covering him. *I've learned my lesson – I'll never, ever be fooled again. I'll go back to how I've always been, on my own, trusting no one.*

Chapter 9

Elliot
"Oh, where are you, Denzil?"

Elliot searched for Denzil all day on Sunday but there was no sign of him anywhere. He had wanted to search for him the previous night too, but his mum hadn't let him. He hardly noticed the snow which had been falling lightly all day. He had to find the dog soon – before he got too far away.

Mum had told him firmly to give up all thoughts of having a dog. "And you're not to have anything more to do with Denzil," she insisted. "You've got to get used to the idea."

But Elliot couldn't give up on Denzil – he had to find him. At least the twins were sympathetic. He bumped into them while he was out searching and they offered to help. That was great – three pairs of eyes had much more chance of spotting the missing dog. Plus it also meant he'd be able to search further afield as Mum didn't like him going far on his own.

"But what will you do with Denzil if we do find him?" asked Kai.

"I don't know," said Elliot, "but I've got to make sure he's all right. And I've got to try and explain to him – he thinks I don't care."

They searched before and after school all the following week. Sometimes, after school, they took Sam along too – hoping he could help to find Denzil. Elliot just told Mum he was with the twins – which, of course, wasn't actually a lie.

It was much colder now and there had been quite a lot more snow, but the three children just trudged through it calling to the missing dog. They searched everywhere they could think of, asked everyone they met but there was no sign of Denzil anywhere. Elliot even checked back at the dogs' home and Angela promised to let him know if the dog wardens picked him up again.

Myles was trying to be nice to him. When Elliot got home on Friday evening he told him he'd got a surprise for him. "I've had the day off work today and I've been very busy."

Elliot spotted the book on the table. *Decorating Made Easy.*

"I've been re-decorating your bedroom and I've stencilled animals all over the walls," he told Elliot. "There's lions, tigers, elephants, kangaroos and bears," he said. "And lots of dogs, of course."

Elliot managed a half-smile. "That's kind of you," he said. At least Myles was trying. He opened the bedroom door. Myles obviously couldn't help being allergic to animals it was just. . .

He stopped in horror. The animals were all bright pinks, blues, reds, yellows and greens. It looked awful! Why couldn't Myles ever get anything right?

"I thought the bright colours would appeal to the baby too," said Myles cheerfully.

Elliot had been finding it difficult to sleep all week, but when he did get to sleep that night he dreamed he was being chased by a bright-red elephant and a green kangaroo with yellow spots.

He was pleased the next day was Saturday, he had the whole day to search for Denzil. He had no luck in the morning and in the afternoon the twins joined him along with Sam, who was straining at his lead, eager to be off.

"Where shall we look today?" asked Abbie. "We've searched just about the whole town now."

"I'm just looking everywhere again," said Elliot. "Denzil won't have stayed in one place and anyway we might have missed him."

It was snowing quite hard as they trudged the streets, calling to Denzil. They searched down alleyways, under hedges and round the back of shops.

They'd reached the other side of town when suddenly two older boys rushed past them. They were sliding on the snow and, as they slid past an old lady, they knocked her bags of shopping out of her hands. They ran off laughing, leaving the old lady with her shopping scattered all over the pavement.

Elliot, Abbie and Kai ran up to her. "Are you all right?" asked Abbie.

"Just a bit shaken," she said, but she looked very upset.

Abbie and Elliot started picking up her shopping for her while Kai held on to Sam who was keen to run after the boys.

The old lady only lived a couple of roads away so they helped her back home with the shopping.

"That's so kind of you, dears," she said, sinking into a chair in her kitchen.

Sam slumped down at her feet so Kai started putting the shopping in the cupboard while Abbie made her a cup of tea.

"You will stay and have a cup with me, won't you?" she asked them.

"Of course we will," said Abbie, getting the milk out of the fridge.

Elliot sighed. The old lady was obviously shaken and no doubt lonely too, so how could they refuse? But he wanted to get on with searching for Denzil. Every day that passed meant the dog could be further away, and it would be getting dark very soon.

Oh where are you, Denzil? he thought desperately.

Chapter 10

Denzil
A Secret Dog

Denzil shifted on his sack on the shed floor. "I'll be glad when this snow stops and I can be on my way," he said to himself.

He'd taken refuge from the snow in a very overgrown and neglected garden. He'd been there all week as Hester, the lady who lived there, left him pretty much alone. She'd even given him some scraps a few times and she never tried to get him into the house – or give him a bath!

He got up for a good scratch. "Hester's OK but I'll never trust another human again. They make you think one thing and then they let you down – big time!"

One good thing about staying here was that it was quite near to a hamburger restaurant. Denzil popped out regularly to find leftovers and once someone even chucked one over the garden wall.

He ambled over to the shed doorway to look out. "The king of the road will be off again soon. All those places to see, all those new smells to sniff –" He stopped as he heard Hester's voice.

"The dog's out here," she said. "He doesn't want to come in the house. I bought that tin of dog food for the poor little chap for a treat."

"Where is he? Is he in that shed?"

The voice was familiar. *It's Elliot!* thought Denzil.

Denzil had heard Elliot calling him several times but he'd kept hidden. Now he was here – Hester was bringing him into the garden.

He'd have to hide. . .

But then Sam was bounding down the garden, barking like mad. He'd spotted him. It was too late.

"Denzil!" Elliot rushed past Sam and threw his arms round him. "Oh, where have you been? I've been looking everywhere for you."

Denzil tried to pull away but Elliot held on to him, hugging him.

Then Elliot pushed the tangled hair back from Denzil's face and looked lovingly into his eyes. "I've been so worried about you. Are you all right?"

He sounds just like he cares about me,

thought Denzil. *Perhaps, he really does care. But then why did he. . .? Oh, I'll never understand humans.*

He saw the two girls that had adopted Sam. They came over and stroked him too, even they looked pleased to see him.

Elliot jumped up to talk to Hester. He sounded very excited. "If Denzil could stay living here with you, I could come twice a day to feed him."

"I'd like that," said Hester. "He's company for me, even though he lives out here, and he doesn't need much looking after. He seems to find most of his own food, hamburgers usually but one day he brought back a whole string of sausages. Goodness knows where he gets it all from."

Elliot laughed. "Oh, this is just great. I'll take him for a walk every day too."

Denzil looked up. *Why does he keep thinking I need taking for a walk? But then, it was fun last time. . .*

"This could prove to be the perfect arrangement for you," said Abbie.

"Yes, but we'll have to keep it a secret," said Elliot. "Mum and Myles will be furious if they find out I've disobeyed them." He quickly explained to Hester what had happened when he'd taken Denzil home.

"Well you won't be harming anyone with him living here," she said. "And it will be lovely for me to have you visiting. It gets a bit lonely here on my own sometimes."

"So it's great all round," said Kai. "We'll come and visit sometimes too. We can take Denzil and Sam for walks together, it will be nice for them."

"We'll have to keep to this side of

town," said Elliot. "I can't risk walking him anywhere near home."

Abbie nodded. "And don't worry, we won't tell anyone about Denzil. He'll be our secret."

Denzil sighed. So he was to be a secret dog. Well, that was OK with him. He had somewhere to live now and it wasn't in a stuffy house, he still had his freedom. He had new friends – and he had Elliot. Being a secret dog sounded just fine to him.

Chapter 11

Elliot
A Close Thing

Elliot had never been so happy. He went to see Denzil every morning, on his way to school and again on the way home. Before he went home every evening, Elliot was careful to thoroughly brush all his clothes to remove the dog hair and to wash his hands.

Mum was pleased to see him smiling again. "I'm glad you've got Abbie and Kai for friends," she told him. "It's doing you good, spending time with them." Elliot knew that what she really meant was it was taking his mind off Denzil. If only she knew!

Elliot bought food for Denzil with his pocket money, although fortunately he didn't need much as he found a lot for himself. One of Elliot's first jobs when he arrived at Hester's in the morning was to clear away the empty hamburger cartons the dog had brought home.

Weekends were the best, taking Denzil for long walks in the park. Abbie and Kai usually came and brought Sam as well.

Hester was happy too and always looked pleased to see them. But all three children were beginning to get worried about her.

"She's not coping very well, is she?" said Kai. "The house hasn't been cleaned properly for ages by the look of it."

"Maybe we could help her," suggested Elliot. "In return for all she's doing for us and for Denzil.

"That's really kind of you," said Hester, when they suggested it. "You don't need to do anything – I love having you here. But if it makes you feel better, well, the place does need a bit of sprucing up."

So on Saturday afternoon they decided to start on the kitchen. Abbie and Kai arrived on their bikes as they didn't have Sam with them. The twins' mum was giving him a bath. They started cleaning the cupboards and the work surfaces.

Elliot concentrated on the cooker and was just standing back to admire his handiwork when he noticed a shelf hanging off the wall. "I could fix that for you," he told Hester. "I've helped my stepfather put up shelves often enough, we put another new one up just last night."

"Not more books?" said Abbie.

Elliot nodded. "A new set of encyclo-paedias this time."

He popped home to borrow some of Myles's tools. Mum was fast asleep on the bed and Myles was out so Elliot didn't have to think of an excuse why he wanted them.

Hopefully he could sneak them back later without Myles even knowing.

He'd almost reached Hester's road when, to his horror, he spotted a familiar figure walking towards him.

"Myles! Oh no! What's he doing round here?"

It was too late to turn back – Myles had spotted him. Elliot hastily hid the bag of tools behind him.

"Elliot!" called Myles, hurrying towards him. "Where are you off to?"

"Just visiting a friend," said Elliot quickly. "Abbie and Kai are waiting for me there. What are you doing round here?"

"I'm just looking round my old territory," said Myles. "I used to live in this road when I was a boy."

Elliot's heart sank – he had no idea Myles had lived round here.

"Haven't been back for years," said Myles. "That was the house we lived in, over there."

Elliot looked where Myles was pointing. The house was just round the corner to Hester's road. "Er – it looks nice," he said.

"Yes, it was," said Myles. "Anyway better get back. I left your mum having a rest."

"See you later then," said Elliot. He breathed a huge sigh of relief as Myles turned to go. If he hadn't been back for years until now then the chances were he wouldn't come back again for a long time.

Elliot walked round the corner and Hester opened the door to him. "I've got the tools," he told her.

"And would they be my tools by any chance?" said a voice behind him.

Elliot spun round. "Myles!" He stared at him in horror. "You – you followed me."

"You looked so worried when you saw me I knew you were up to something," said Myles. "And I wondered what you were hiding behind your back."

"I – er. . ." started Elliot but Myles was

looking up at the house. Then he switched to staring at Hester.

"Good heavens," he said. "It can't be – can it? Hester Brannon?"

"Well, yes," said Hester. "But – wait a minute. It's Myles, isn't it?"

Myles grinned and nodded. "I thought you'd gone to New Zealand with the rest of the family," he said.

Elliot was speechless. Myles and Hester knew each other. A thousand thoughts were whizzing round in his head and most of them involved Denzil.

"I changed my mind about New Zealand, pretty much at the last minute," said Hester. "I didn't want to leave England. Didn't Robert write and tell you?"

Myles chuckled. "No, Robert didn't get round to writing. He did say he wasn't much good at it before he left. We've lost touch now." He turned to Elliot. "Hester's son and I grew up together."

"Always round here, he was," Hester joined in. "Right pair of tearaways."

Elliot couldn't imagine Myles as a "tearaway" but he thought it was time he warned Hester who he was. "Myles is my stepfather," he told her.

Hester thought for a minute then gave him a knowing wink – she understood. "Elliot has been helping me," she told Myles. "He and the twins often come to give me a hand."

Good old Hester, thought Elliot. *She might be getting old, but she's pretty quick to pick up on the situation.*

Myles looked back at Elliot. "Why didn't you tell us? It's wonderful that you're helping Hester. There was no need to keep it a secret."

"Well – er I don't know really," said Elliot. He could feel himself going red in the face. "I'm sorry I took your tools without asking you but I wanted to fix Hester's kitchen shelf."

"Oh, I'll do that for you," said Myles, stepping into the hall. "The kitchen's this way, if I remember rightly."

Elliot nervously followed him along the hall to the kitchen. If Denzil stayed in his shed Myles shouldn't be able to see him through the window.

Myles looked at the shelf. "This won't take long."

Elliot passed him his tools and then looked over at Kai who was obviously holding her breath as she watched Myles.

Elliot tilted his head towards the garden and mouthed the word *Denzil* to her.

She nodded to him and slipped outside to keep Denzil out of sight.

Myles was getting quite good at shelves now and the job didn't take long, even though he was chatting to Hester about "the old days" all the time.

"It's very kind of you, Myles," said Hester. "And it is good to see you again – just wait till I tell Robert next time he phones."

"Do give him my best," said Myles. "Is there anything else I can do for you? I could come back. . ."

"No," said Elliot quickly. "Everything's fine, isn't it, Hester?"

Myles looked a bit surprised.

"I'm coping perfectly well, dear," said Hester. "And Elliot and the twins keep me company. Why don't you give me a ring sometime? I'd like that."

Myles smiled at her. "Of course I will." He jotted down Hester's number and Robert's number in New Zealand.

Elliot was anxious to get Myles away from Hester's as soon as possible. "I'll walk back with you," he told him. "It's nearly tea time."

He breathed a sigh of relief as they left. It had been a close thing but he'd got away with it – this time.

Chapter 12

Denzil

Something's Wrong With Hester!

Denzil had watched the sneezing man arrive through the fence, so his sixth sense had told him to keep out of the way. He hadn't actually needed Kai to come out and explain. *But it was pretty good of her,* he thought. *She obviously didn't realize that a streetwise dog like me soon picks up on what's what.*

He watched her and Abbie leave on their bikes just after Elliot and the sneezing man. *I hope they bring Sam with them again next time,* he thought.

Then Hester came out to give him the dog food that Elliot had brought him. But she didn't seem quite right. She seemed distant somehow.

"What's the matter, Hester?" he barked. But of course she couldn't understand him.

Suddenly, she fell right to the ground in front of him. Denzil jumped back as the bowl of food crashed beside him.

Hester didn't get up. She just laid there on the cold ground and her body was twitching.

Denzil rushed to lick her face. Then he tried to rouse her with his nose. She didn't stir. "Hester! Hester!" he barked. "Wake up. Please get up." Nothing made any difference.

There was only one thing he could do. He'd have to get Elliot.

Elliot's scent was still fresh. *Here goes the bloodhound bit of me again,* he thought, as he raced along after him. *Good job I've got some greyhound in me too.*

He caught up with him just a couple of streets away. "Elliot!" he barked. "Elliot!"

Elliot turned round. He didn't look pleased to see Denzil at all. But there was no time to worry about that, he had to get him back to help Hester.

The sneezing man had gone all red again but he didn't start sneezing. "Where did that dog come from?" he shouted at Elliot.

Denzil barked impatiently at him. This was no time for arguing.

He jumped up and tugged on Elliot's coat sleeve. Then he ran a little way in the direction of Hester's and then back to Elliot. He repeated this a couple of times.

Elliot got the message. "There must be something wrong with Hester," he cried. "I've got to go back."

Denzil raced ahead with Elliot and the sneezing man following. He led them straight into the garden and was relieved to find Hester sitting up. She looked a bit dazed.

Thank goodness, thought Denzil, and ran to lick her face.

"Get that dog away from her," shouted the sneezing man.

What a cheek! thought Denzil, as Elliot pulled him away and the man bent down himself to look at Hester.

"I think it was just a fit," she told him shakily. "I haven't had one for ages but I must admit, I don't always remember to take my tablets lately."

"Well, I think you should be checked out by your doctor," he said, helping her to her feet.

He turned on Elliot. "So that's why you didn't want me to come back – you've been hiding your dog here, haven't you?"

Elliot nodded miserably. "But Denzil doesn't affect you here. I'm not doing any harm."

"You disobeyed your mother and me," said the sneezing man. "Just how long did you think you could keep it a secret? You must have known we'd find out eventually."

Then Hester spoke up. "Denzil actually arrived on his own and Elliot found him here," she said. "I'm happy to let the dog stay and Elliot takes care of him. He and the twins have been such a help to me."

"Yes, well that's not the point," said the man, leading her towards the house. Elliot followed them in and Denzil jumped up to look in the window.

The man had taken Hester into the sitting room and was looking round at the dust and cobwebs and the piles of stuff everywhere. "Oh dear, you're just not coping, are you, Hester? You really shouldn't be living here alone, especially as you're forgetting to take your tablets."

He pushed some papers aside and sat her down gently on the settee. "Don't you think you'd be better looked after in an old people's home?"

"She can't go into a home," cried Elliot.

Denzil was equally horrified. *No, she can't go into a home,* he thought. *Not an old lady like her. She couldn't possibly cope with living in one of those tiny kennels with just a bowl of food and water twice a day. Or with being turned out into a freezing cold run every morning.*

Denzil knew only too well what it was like. *And those baskets are much too small for her to sleep in,* he thought.

Chapter 13

Elliot
A Plan

Back at the flat that evening, while Myles was reading in the bedroom, Elliot complained bitterly to his mother. "Myles is ruining everything," he cried.

"No he's not, he's doing what's right," said Mum. "From what he told me, I have to agree with him that Hester would be better off in a home."

"But she doesn't want to go into a home," said Elliot. "She likes living there – and she likes having Denzil there too."

"You mustn't be selfish," said Mum. "Hester needs help."

"But we were helping her," argued Elliot. "Before Myles interfered. You can't make her go into a home."

"It's not up to us," said Mum. "Myles has phoned Hester's son in New Zealand and he's coming over to sort his mother out."

She made it plain that she didn't want to discuss it any more. She'd been furious with Elliot for disobeying her about Denzil, and Myles had warned him not to upset her any more. The baby was due very soon.

At least Mum didn't try to stop Elliot from visiting Denzil and Hester. She even went with him a couple of times to see Hester herself.

Elliot continued to go every day and

Mum sometimes sent a pie or a home-made cake for the old lady. Myles was busy working overtime at the bookshop, as they were stocktaking, but he phoned Hester regularly.

Elliot had come up with a plan. He eagerly explained it to Abbie and Kai. "If we can get Hester's house clean and tidy before her son comes from New Zealand, then he'll see she can cope on her own – at least with our help."

"Yes, and if we remind her to take her tablets every day," said Abbie. "She might not have any more fits."

Hester was in full agreement with all this.

The three children worked very hard. It was a large house and they cleaned, polished, vacuumed, tidied and washed floors and curtains. And Elliot still found time to feed and walk Denzil.

"I'm sure it's going to work," said Kai. "Hester's son is bound to be impressed."

"Robert's arriving on Saturday," Hester told them. "He phoned me this morning."

"That's great," said Elliot. "Myles will be working in the bookshop this Saturday. So we'll get to him first." Things were looking hopeful.

But on Friday evening, when Elliot got home, a tall dark-haired man was sitting on the sofa with Myles. "This is Robert, Hester's son," Myles told Elliot.

"What? But you're not coming till tomorrow – you told Hester."

"I told Hester I would be going to see her tomorrow," said Robert. "But Myles wanted a word with me first."

Elliot turned on Myles. He was sick of his interfering. "How could you? You haven't given Hester a chance." He was never, ever going to speak to him again.

"Hey, don't get upset," said Robert. "I've been concerned for some time that my mother wasn't coping on her own. I'd got a good idea from her letters and phone calls."

"But she is coping now," cried Elliot. "With our help. You've got to go and look – the house is all cleaned and tidied up."

"Well that's good," said Robert. "It'll make it all the nicer for you to move in to."

"What?" Elliot looked round at his

mother, who was smiling at him, and then at Myles and then back to Robert "But how can we. . .?"

"That's what Myles wanted to talk to me about," Robert explained. "He suggested to me that you all move in with Hester to take care of her. There's plenty of room."

Myles's eyes glinted behind his glasses. "We didn't want to tell you in case it didn't work out," he told Elliot, with a big grin. "You'll have to help out of course – your mother will be busy with the new baby. But then you've been doing that already. And you'll have your own room there."

"Hester only really needs keeping an eye on at the moment," said Mum. "And later, when she needs more care, the baby will be older and I am a trained nurse so I'll be able to manage."

Elliot couldn't believe it. "But Hester—"

"—has already agreed," said Robert. "I've just spoken to her on the phone, while you were walking home. She's over the moon with the idea."

Elliot's mind was whirring – they'd be living in a house – with a garden – just like he'd always wanted. Myles had fixed it. But with Myles there. . .

"Oh no, what about Denzil?"

Myles came over to him and put his hand on his shoulder. "He can stay," he told him softly.

"But your allergy."

"He only affects me if he's indoors with me," said Myles. "Where the air is concentrated. As long as he stays outside in the fresh air, and I don't get too close, I'm OK. You must have noticed, I didn't sneeze once when I was in Hester's garden."

"Yes! And Denzil prefers to be outside," cried Elliot. "He won't be any trouble – I promise."

"He's a bright dog," said Myles. "Amazing how he came to get you when Hester was in trouble."

Elliot couldn't believe it. He didn't stop to think about it, he threw his arms round Myles's neck and hugged him. Then he hugged his mother and then Robert. Robert laughed in surprise. "I can't wait to tell Denzil tomorrow," said Elliot.

Chapter 14

Denzil
Something's Going On

Denzil wondered what was happening.
Hester had brought a strange man called
Robert out to see him first thing in the
morning. She seemed to like him a lot.

*I guess he must be all right, if Hester
likes him,* Denzil thought to himself, and
he'd allowed Robert to stroke him. As
soon as he'd gone back inside, Denzil
had settled down to finish off last night's
hamburger.

Then Elliot had opened the back gate.
"Denzil. Guess what?"

But the sneezing man and the lady with the big tummy were with him too. The man grabbed Elliot's arm and pulled him back.

"Come and talk to Hester first," he said. "It's only polite."

"I'll be back in a minute," Elliot called to Denzil. "I've got something to tell you."

Denzil was just wondering what it could be when Abbie and Kai came round the back with Sam.

They left Sam in the garden with Denzil, then went into the house carrying some clean curtains.

"Something's going on," said Denzil.

"Everything seems fine to me," said Sam.

"Yes, well you haven't got razor sharp senses like me," said Denzil. "You've never been a dog of the road and had to fend for yourself. I've learned to be suspicious – always."

"Oh, come on. . ."

But Denzil wasn't listening. He trotted over to the house and stood up on his large back feet to look in the sitting-room window.

"Abbie and Kai are hanging up the curtains," he told Sam. "But the others are all talking."

"So? Humans do a lot of talking."

"So – I don't know – they all seem excited."

Sam jumped up to join him and peered in too. "Well, that's good, isn't it?"

"Not necessarily good for us," said Denzil. He tilted his head and strained his ears to hear what they were saying.

"I thought that you could have the bedroom at the back, Elliot," said Hester. "It overlooks the garden."

Bedroom? thought Denzil. *That's where humans sleep.*

"And you and Myles can have the big front room," Hester said to the lady with the big tummy. "And the small room next to it will be just right for the baby."

"What baby?" asked Denzil.

"I don't know," said Sam. "What's a baby anyway?"

"It's a human puppy," said Denzil.

Now Robert was speaking to them. "Mother and I won't be charging you any rent for living here, in return for looking after everything," he said. "That will give you a chance to save some money. Then, when you've got enough for a deposit, you might be able to get a loan and buy the house from us – eventually."

"Oh that's just wonderful," cried the lady with the big tummy. She put her arms round Hester. "Thank you, my dear. You won't have to worry about a thing – I promise you, you'll be taken very good care of."

"I don't believe it! They're moving in here," said Denzil. "They're putting Hester in a home to be taken care of and moving in themselves. And Hester seems to have agreed!"

"Why?" asked Sam.

"I don't know everything," said Denzil irritably.

Then Abbie and Kai said goodbye to everyone and came outside to get Sam. "Well, it looks like my family's not moving in here anyway," said Sam. He jumped down to join the twins.

Denzil nodded and watched him trot off with them. *What's going to happen now?* he thought. He knew the sneezing man didn't like him anywhere near him. And the man had even told Elliot to get him away from Hester when she'd fallen. If he was moving in, then what. . .?

Elliot was talking now so Denzil cocked his head the other way to hear better. "And it's all due to Denzil," said Elliot.

He was getting the blame for something. *What have I done?* he wondered. *And why would Elliot blame me? I thought he loved me.*

Everyone was nodding in agreement but then the excitement appeared to be too much for the lady with the big tummy.

She suddenly clutched her stomach and started groaning.

"The baby's coming," she cried.

Where? Denzil looked around him.

The sneezing man grabbed hold of the lady. "Come on, we'd better get you straight off to St Anthony's."

Is he taking her off to a home too? Maybe he's cross with her because she's making a fuss.

Denzil jumped down and ran round the side just in time to see them come out of the front.

"I'll drive you there," said Robert, opening a car door.

The sneezing man helped the lady inside then shouted at Elliot to hurry up.

Denzil was worried. He barked at Elliot to come and tell him what was happening.

"I must just tell Denzil about his home," said Elliot.

"There's no time," said the sneezing man. "Get into the car. We'll sort Denzil out later."

Oh no he won't! thought Denzil. *I'm not waiting around to be sent back to the home. I'm off.*

He briefly considered taking Hester with him too but he realized that an old lady like her couldn't possibly cope with life on the road. So he reluctantly left her behind as he plodded off down the street.

He'd been right all along – you could only trust yourself. "Why didn't I learn my lesson the first time Elliot let me down?" he asked himself. "Well, I'll make sure he never finds me again."

He turned into the park and stopped to

check a couple of bushes for new smells. Then he had a drink from the pond. At least it wasn't frozen over and it tasted good. The water that humans gave you just didn't taste the same.

He sniffed the fresh air. "This is the life," he said. "Freedom. My own boss – no one to worry about except myself. King of the road again." This was how he really wanted to be.

He paused for a moment. If this was how he really wanted to be, then why did he feel so miserable?

Chapter 15

Elliot
Where's Denzil?

The baby – Bethany Jane – was finally born at six o'clock the following morning. And she didn't look a bit like a miniature Myles. In fact they said she had Elliot's nose.

Elliot was exhausted. He'd been up all night – they all had. The strange thing was, Mum didn't look tired at all now, sitting up holding Bethany.

But Myles insisted that she should rest now. "I'll take Elliot home and get us both some breakfast," he told her. Then he went off to call a taxi.

Elliot kissed his mother, and then Bethany. Bethany was really cute. He was surprised – he hadn't expected to actually *like* the baby.

Elliot felt very happy as they left the hospital, everything had worked out so well. It had been snowing again in the night and everywhere was covered with a fresh, white blanket. It seemed almost magical.

"Can we go and tell Denzil about us moving in and him staying too?" he asked Myles, as the taxi drew up.

Myles laughed as he opened the door. "All right. But he is only a dog, you know. He can't understand you."

Elliot didn't bother to argue. He *knew* Denzil understood him.

The taxi dropped them outside Hester's and Elliot rushed straight round to the back garden. "Denzil! Denzil. Guess what?" But there was no sign of the scruffy dog in the garden or the shed.

"Maybe he's gone out to get himself something to eat," said Elliot. Then Myles and Hester came out to see him.

"I'm sorry, Elliot," said Hester. "But Denzil left just after you yesterday and he hasn't been back."

"But that was ages ago," cried Elliot. "Something must have happened to him. I've got to find him."

"But, Elliot, we've had no sleep," started Myles.

"I don't care – and you don't have to come." He was already at the gate now.

"No, wait," said Myles. "I'll help you."

Elliot was surprised but very glad of the support.

They went out into the street together. "He's been gone some time," said Myles. "He could be anywhere."

"He might be lying injured somewhere," said Elliot. He couldn't bear the thought of the poor dog hurt and alone.

They started checking round the parked cars and over walls and fences into people's front gardens. There was no sign of the scruffy dog in any of the nearby streets.

"If only it hadn't snowed again," said Elliot. "We could have followed his footprints."

Then they checked round the hamburger restaurant and the back of the local shops but he wasn't there either.

"Where else did he like to go?" asked Myles.

"He liked the park," said Elliot.

So they made their way towards the park, calling him all the time.

They searched under bushes, behind trees and asked everyone they met if they'd seen him, but no one had. There was no shortage of doggy footprints in the park but, of course, any of the larger ones could have been Denzil's.

It was really cold and they stamped their feet to keep themselves warm. Myles sniffed the air and grinned. "Maybe I'll start sneezing – then we'll know we're close."

"But it doesn't affect you in the open air," said Elliot. He knew Myles was attempting to cheer him up with his joke but he couldn't even smile.

"I do actually like dogs," Myles told him, as they investigated yet another bush. "It's just this allergy – and there aren't many places you can keep a dog outside. Plus most dogs wouldn't want to live outside – it wouldn't be kind."

"No, Denzil's different," said Elliot. "He's just – perfect. . ." He almost choked on the last word.

Myles put his arm round his shoulders. "Come on, we haven't looked over here yet."

They moved off to search yet more bushes and trees.

It was almost lunchtime when Myles said, "I'm sorry, Elliot, but I've got to go back to the hospital this afternoon. And I really do think we need something hot to eat and drink."

"That's all right, you go," said Elliot. He'd been surprised and grateful that Myles had helped him at all. "Mum will want to see you and I know you'll want to be with Bethany."

He looked round at the big expanse of white. It looked hopeless – Denzil could be anywhere – even miles away by now. He felt so alone. Mum had the baby now and Myles was bound to be more interested in his own daughter than him. And he – Elliot – didn't have Denzil any more.

"Look, Bethany isn't going to be more important than you," said Myles, as if he knew what he was thinking. "I know I'm not your real dad and I know I don't always get things right. But I do think of you as my son and we're mates as well, right? After all, you're my right-hand man for putting up shelves."

Elliot nodded. Myles was really trying.

"I'll stay another half an hour if you like," Myles offered.

"Thanks." Elliot managed a smile. "Denzil's obviously not in the park, so we might as well look somewhere else."

They made their way towards the park gates.

Chapter 16

Denzil
"I love you, Denzil."

Denzil watched Elliot and the sneezing man from inside his bush. *Why are they bothering to look for me?* he wondered. *Are they really that keen to get me back in the home? The man's obsessed! He's obviously taken the lady with the big tummy to one as she's not with them now.*

He was cold and miserable. Even the hamburgers he'd collected last night hadn't cheered him up. "I was fine before I got tangled up with humans," he growled to himself. "Never, ever again."

At least it looked as if they were going now. Denzil shrank back further into the darkness of his bush as they walked past.

Then the sneezing man kicked something in the snow and stooped to pick it up. "Look at this," he said to Elliot. "A hamburger carton. It's disgraceful the way people drop litter."

He's always moaning, thought Denzil. *How am I supposed to get them in the litter bin?*

"And here's another one," said the sneezing man, gathering it up. "And another. Have people actually been having a picnic in the snow?"

"Hamburgers!" cried Elliot, taking the carton from him.

"Er – yes, Elliot." The sneezing man looked puzzled.

"Don't you see?" cried Elliot. "Hamburgers – Denzil – he loves them. Look, there's even teeth marks on this carton. He's got to be here somewhere."

Denzil tried to back out of the bush but there was a big branch behind him, stopping him. Then Elliot was on his hands and knees in the snow, peering into the bush.

"Denzil! You're here." Elliot parted the branches and tried to crawl in to him.

The sneezing man stopped him. "Better get him to come out," he said. "It's dangerous to make an animal feel trapped. I read it in one of my books."

Feel trapped? thought Denzil. *That's exactly what he's trying to do – trap me in a home.*

"Denzil, please come out," Elliot coaxed.

117

"Why did you run away? Did you think I'd left you? I wouldn't have – I just didn't get a chance to tell you everything."

Denzil didn't move. *You're not fooling me again*, he thought.

"And guess what?" said Elliot. "You don't make Myles sneeze when you're outside."

Me? thought Denzil. *What's it got to do with me? Why do I always get the blame?*

"Oh, come on, Denzil," Elliot pleaded. "We're all going to be together now. You, me, Hester, Myles, Mum and the new baby – one big family. Myles has fixed it. We're never going to be parted again – not ever. I promise you."

The sneezing man bent down towards him, although he seemed to be keeping his distance. "I'll even give you one of my home-made hamburgers," he told him.

Denzil wasn't sure he trusted him – even with the offer of hamburgers. But then he looked into Elliot's eyes. You could tell a lot by people's eyes. Elliot looked sincere, loving. *Real soulful eyes*, he thought.

He decided to venture out slowly.

Elliot immediately hugged him, then he brushed some snow off his face, then hugged him again. "Oh, I love you, Denzil."

Even the sneezing man was smiling. Denzil didn't understand quite what was going on but he now knew for certain the most important thing – that Elliot loved him. Somehow that was all that mattered and he didn't mind who came to live with them – even this baby everyone kept talking about – just as long as he was with Elliot.

"Come on, boy," said Elliot, and Denzil followed him, boy and dog happily running and jumping through the snow together.

"You know what, Denzil?" Elliot called to him. "You really are the best dog in the world."

The Best
Christmas
Ever

Chapter 1

I'm Not Staying Here!

"They might want to stay in that strange house. But I don't." With two leaps and a bound Puss was across the few paving slabs they called a front garden.

"I'm off home – before Ginger Tom takes over my territory. All that time and effort I put into defending it. . . How dare they take me away."

The sudden noise of the traffic was deafening as Puss skidded round on to the pavement. He kept his head down and ran. Round the corner and round the next. Over a wall and across a garden.

"And as for shoving me in that basket. . ." His ears twitched at the indignity of it. He was only usually put in THAT basket to go to someone called Vet. Puss didn't like that either but at least you got to go home again after Vet had stuck needles in you.

"Which way?" He leapt on to a high wooden fence and sniffed the air for familiar smells. "Ah-choo!" The traffic fumes were getting up his nose. "How can you smell anything round here?"

His long black tail swished from side to side as he looked up and down the street. "Houses. Nothing but houses. Where are the fields? Where are the trees?"

He cringed as yet another lorry thundered by. "Ye-owl!" Puss was used to a few cars coming through his village but this was dreadful – they never stopped. "Why on earth did Jenni want to come and live HERE?"

He spotted a tabby cat sitting on the bonnet of a red car that was parked in a front garden. "I'll ask him where the fields are."

Puss jumped down and padded over to the cat, his tail gently curved in a friendly manner. "Excuse me." He thought he'd better be polite – after all he was a stranger here.

The tabby cat immediately stood up and arched his back. His fur bristled to the end of his tail. "Ssss-stay back! Keep your distance!" he spat. "Don't even think about trying to take over my territory."

Puss jumped back. "How rude." No cat in his village would have DARED to speak

to him like that. They knew their place –
they respected him. Well, Ginger Tom did
try it on sometimes – but he soon sorted
him out.

"Call that a territory?" Puss gave the
hissing, spitting cat his Special Stare.
"What would I want with a tiny patch of
gravel with a car parked on it?" he growled.
"And only one measly bush? You should
see my territory – it's ENORMOUS. It's
got LOADS of bushes. And trees to climb
and lots of grass. . ."

The tabby cat wasn't interested. He
crouched down and let out a low, warning
yowl.

Puss gave an irritated flick of his tail.
"It's no use asking HIM anything. He's
obviously got no idea about the finer things
in life."

With his head held high, he stalked off. Puss – the fearless cat – had never needed anybody's help before. "And I don't need it now," he said.

Round the corner there was a row of different buildings. Puss stared up at the big windows full of gold and glitter.

"Shops." He'd only ever seen the village shops from the car on the way to see Vet. And he'd never taken much notice – he was too busy sulking at having been shoved in THAT basket again. But he knew about the shops – that was where Jenni's mum got his cat food.

He broke into a run. "The fields will be just up here. And then I'll be home."

He gradually slowed down as he got past the shops. There were no fields. Just more houses.

These were not the village shops.

He kept walking, ears pricked for familiar sounds. "How can I hear the cows mooing or the field mice squeaking with all this traffic?"

He glanced down to check his white front feet. His boots, Jenni called them. She often called him Puss in Boots because he was all black with four white feet. His boots were definitely looking grubby but he couldn't stop to wash them now.

"They actually expected me to STAY at that house," he grumbled. "Telling me I had to get used to it and then I could go out in the back garden. Call that a back garden? That tiny square of grass I saw from the window? Huh! I'm going back to my OWN garden – my OWN territory."

He stopped and looked all around him.

Nothing was familiar – he couldn't see anything he recognized.

Then, through the traffic, he caught a glimpse of something ginger on the other side of the road. It was a cat.

"It's Ginger Tom!" cried Puss. He actually felt pleased to see him. "If he's here then home must be just around the corner. I bet he's on his way to try and take over my territory right now. I'll show him."

He tried to get across the road to him. But the traffic just didn't stop. There was only one thing for it. He put his head down and made a dash for it.

There was a terrific squeal of brakes. Horns tooted. A man fell off his bike and shouted at him – Puss had never been called THAT before!

Somehow, he made it to the other pavement. He was breathing hard and his heart was beating fast. The cat was sitting on a fence watching him.

It wasn't Ginger Tom.

Chapter 2

Where Are You, Puss?

"Puss! Puss!" Jenni's throat was getting sore from calling. "Oh, where can he have got to?"

"I should have checked those boxes before I opened the door," said her mother. "I know how Puss likes boxes. But the way he shot out – so fast – it was almost as though he'd planned it."

"He probably had," said Jenni. "He hates being shut in. If only he'd waited till he was used to his new home. Now the poor little thing's got himself lost."

Jenny's mother shivered in the cold December air. "We've been searching for two hours now. I think we should go back and have a hot drink."

"No. You go back if you want to," said Jenni. "I've got to keep looking for him."

"But you'll get lost too, on your own," said her mother. "We haven't even been in East Deeming for two whole days yet."

"I'll be okay," said Jenni. "All I have to do is look for that really tall office block and I know our house is just round the corner."

As she set off again she looked at all the unfriendly people who just walked by without speaking to anyone. In the small village where they'd lived before everyone knew each other and stopped to say, "Good morning" or "How are you today?"

She knew Dad felt bad about them

having to leave their village – and all their friends. But he'd had to move with his job. It wasn't his fault.

"Puss. Puss," she called, for probably the five-hundredth time. She passed two girls about the same age as her walking along chatting together.

The children round here have already got their own friends, she thought. I'm dreading starting my new school after Christmas. I wish I wasn't so shy.

In the next road she spotted a tabby cat, sitting on the bonnet of a red car. It stood up for her to stroke it.

"Hello," said Jenni. "You're a nice friendly cat. I wonder if you've seen Puss. If only you could talk."

She walked on looking into all the tiny front gardens. She peered under all the parked cars. Everywhere felt so strange – so closed in. She missed the big open fields – and all the animals.

"I shouldn't think there are any animals living round here – apart from the odd cat or dog," she said to herself. "I so loved helping Mr Roberts get his cows in for milking. And collecting the eggs with Anna – and feeding the chickens and geese." She gave a big sigh. "There's nothing to do round here."

Just round the corner was a row of shops. The windows were bright with Christmas decorations. But they did nothing to cheer her up.

Jenni shivered. "Perhaps I should go back for a hot drink. And maybe – just maybe – I'll find Puss has come home on his own."

But Puss wasn't at home.

Jenni's mother had gone back to unpacking the huge boxes of their belongings. She was anxious to get the house straight before she started her new job after Christmas.

Jenni begged her to phone the people that had bought their house in the country. "You do hear of cats and dogs turning up at their old homes," she said.

"I know you do, dear," said her mother. "But we've moved over three hundred kilometres. He might be a clever cat, but even Puss couldn't find his way back there."

Jenni quickly swallowed a cup of hot chocolate and opened the front door to go out again. A movement caught her eye. It was a pigeon pecking at something in the road. Jenni watched in amazement as it expertly side-stepped the cars.

"Wow! All this traffic obviously doesn't bother you," Jenni said to it. "But there can't be anything for you to eat round here."

She fetched it some bread and the pigeon raced towards it. He hungrily gobbled it all up and even took a piece from her hand.

Jenni smiled. "At least something is friendly round here," she said.

"We'll all make new friends eventually," said her mother. "And try not to worry too much about Puss. I bet he's trying to find his way back here right now."

Chapter 3

An Even Worse Place Than
Jenni's New House

"The sooner I get away from this dreadful place the better." Puss padded through the big shopping precinct and the mass of human legs. He knew these shops DEFINITELY weren't the ones in the village. These were HUGE. And one of them even had stairs that moved up and down all on their own!

"Ye-owl!" Puss put his ears back and scampered past. "That's not natural."

Puss was hungry. His long black tail swished from side to side. "Not one mouse to catch round here. This is no place for a fearless hunter like me."

There were people everywhere. He padded along trying to dodge the hurrying boots and shoes. "Miaow. Watch where you're putting your big feet. Mind my beautiful tail." But at least there weren't any cars or lorries here.

A movement in a low shop window caught his eye. He stood up on his back feet to get a better look. "Wow! Puppies. And kittens. And birds."

A little brown puppy with a black nose looked up at him. Several others were asleep on top of each other. "What are you doing in there?" asked Puss. "And why are you shut up in cages? Is this some sort of animal prison?"

The puppy obviously couldn't hear him

through the glass. Puss watched a guinea pig in the next cage scurry round in the sawdust to hide behind its brother.

The door opened and a lady came out with a boy who was carefully carrying a small box. "Thanks for buying me this mouse, Mum," he said.

Puss pricked up his ears. She'd bought him a mouse! You had to pay for them round here! No wonder he couldn't find any.

The boy spotted him. "Look, Mum," he said. "D'you think that cat has escaped from the pet shop?"

Puss didn't wait to hear any more. "I'm off. I'm not going to be taken in THERE. They're not shutting me up in a cage – and I've got no money to pay for mice."

There were fewer people about now and it was starting to get dark. Puss turned into an alley behind the brightly-lit shops. His eyes quickly adjusted to the darkness and he spotted some cardboard boxes. "I'll curl up in one for a while, keep warm and have a rest."

But there was someone there. Inside a large box, on its side, Puss saw a young man lying covered up with an old blanket.

"What's he doing? It looks as though he's in bed. Surely he can't live HERE? This is an even worse place than Jenni's new house."

He watched the young man take something out of a bag and begin to eat it. Puss's sensitive nose twitched. He could smell cheese. He liked cheese.

The young man looked up and spotted him. "What's up, mate? You not got anywhere to go either?"

He looked nice – and the cheese smelt good. Puss ventured closer.

"Are you hungry?" The young man broke off a piece and held it out. "It's only a stale old cheese sandwich. It's a bit hard but if you're as hungry as me you'll eat anything."

Puss cautiously took the piece in his mouth. He'd never had a sandwich before. He watched the young man carefully as he chewed on it. It tasted okay.

They finished the sandwich between them and the young man patted the blanket. "Come on. We can keep each other warm."

Puss snuggled up to him in the cardboard

box. In this cold unfriendly place at least there was someone kind – and warm.

When he woke up the next morning, just for a minute, Puss thought he was back home curled up with Jenni. Then the young man moved him to get up and he felt the cold. He blinked at the bleak alley-way.

The young man folded his blanket and picked up his bag. He stroked Puss. "I'm off now. Goodbye, mate. Thanks for the company." He walked to the end of the alley and stopped to look in some dustbins. Then he was gone.

Two scruffy-looking cats sauntered up to the dustbins. Puss darted back into the box and peered out at them. One had long matted black fur and a torn ear. He jumped up and knocked the lid off one of the bins.

It clattered to the ground and both cats leapt in.

The scruffy tortoiseshell cat, which had no tail, jumped out with something in its mouth. It was bacon – Puss could smell it. Then the black one followed with some fish.

Puss watched in amazement as they tore at their meal, looking round them all the time. The young man had looked in the dustbins too before he left. "Is this the way you eat in towns? And you have to pay for the mice. This place gets worse all the time."

Puss edged out a little and sniffed the air again. The bacon smelt good. His mouth watered. "But I'd NEVER lower myself to eat out of a dustbin. It's too degrading."

The two cats suddenly spotted him.

They hissed at him. "Ssss-stay back. This is ours."

This was obviously their territory. Puss retreated into his box – the fearless cat wasn't in the mood for a fight this morning. "Of course, I could beat the two of them easily – if I wanted to."

The two cats eventually left. Puss didn't even stop to think about it – he raced over and leapt into the bin. He found a kipper head, which was quite tasty, and then half a sausage, but that tasted of soap powder.

Crash!

He nearly jumped out of his fur as the other dustbin crashed to the ground.

Puss cautiously peered over the top of his bin.

It wasn't the two cats back. "It's a fox!"

He prepared to run. Then he realized the fox wasn't taking any notice of him. It was tucking into some vegetable peelings that had spilled out of the bin.

"Yuck!" said Puss. "Foxes never do have good taste." He decided to make his escape and jump down while it was busy eating.

But the fox glanced up at Puss, and then it moved over so he could join him. Puss was amazed. The foxes in the country hadn't been friendly at all.

They ate side by side as Puss discovered some tasty bits of cheese rind and a half-eaten hamburger. The hamburger took a lot of chewing – Puss wasn't surprised it was only half eaten.

He felt quite good after his meal. "Now I'm going to find my territory." Beyond the dustbins he could see the shopping precinct

where he had been the night before –
but at the other end of the alley, in the
distance. . .

"A tree," cried Puss. "I'm almost
home."

He bounded off towards it, leaving the
fox to finish his breakfast on his own.

Chapter 4

I Didn't Know You Got Wildlife in Towns

Jenni had missed Puss's soft damp nose being thrust into her face as usual to wake her up in the morning. Not that she'd slept – thinking about him out in the cold, lost and hungry.

She shivered in the early morning cold. The shops weren't open yet in the shopping precinct but several people were scurrying off to work. A movement in an alley caught her eye.

"A fox," she breathed. She stood and watched it eating from an overturned dustbin. "It's beautiful."

The fox had spotted her and was watching her carefully but it kept on eating. Jenni was amazed to be so close to a wild creature. The foxes in the country hardly ever came near the houses and were very shy of humans.

Jenni took a poster out of her bag. She'd made it yesterday evening on the computer and run off twenty-five copies. Even though people weren't friendly round here, she hoped they'd read them and contact her if they spotted Puss.

She'd headed the poster PUSS IN BOOTS in big black letters to give an immediate description of the little black cat with four white feet.

A woman stopped to look at it. "Are you in it too?" she asked.

She took Jenni by surprise. "Pardon?"

"The pantomime – *Puss in Boots*. I haven't seen you at rehearsals."

"Er – no. I'm not," said Jenni.

"Didn't think I'd seen you," said the woman. "Just helping out with the posters, are you?"

She didn't wait for a reply but hurried off.

"I don't believe it," cried Jenni. "Someone's putting on the pantomime *Puss in Boots*. People will just think my posters are an advert for the pantomime." She looked at the poster. Why did they have to be doing *Puss in Boots*? Why couldn't it have been *Cinderella* or *Aladdin*?

Then she had an idea and folded over the top bit with PUSS IN BOOTS on. "It's not so eye-catching but it still makes sense," she decided.

"Lost. Black cat with four white feet," read a voice over her shoulder. She turned to see a woman peering at the poster. "That your cat, love?"

"Yes," said Jenni.

"I'll keep a look out for him," said the woman. "And have you thought of asking your neighbours to check their sheds? He could be shut in somewhere." Then she was gone. But two people had actually spoken to her!

"I'll ask Dad to come with me this evening to knock on all the neighbours' doors," Jenni decided.

She went back and adjusted the posters she had already put up. Then she stuck the rest of them up around the town. A pet shop in the shopping precinct put the last one in their window for her.

On the way home for lunch she spotted a neighbour just coming out of her house carrying a pile of Christmas presents.

Jenni didn't even stop to think about being shy. "Excuse me," she said. "I've lost my black and white cat, and I was wondering if you could look in your garden and in your shed – if you've got one."

"Of course I will," said the woman. "My own cat went missing last year but she turned up at the animal shelter in Sycamore Street. Have you tried there?"

"No," said Jenni. "I didn't know about it. Thank you."

The animal shelter was housed in a large, old, dingy building but inside it looked surprisingly bright and cheerful.

Jenni stood silently with her fingers

crossed on both hands as the receptionist checked their records.

She finally looked up. "No. I'm sorry, your cat hasn't been brought in here." She smiled at Jenni's sad face. "I'll make a note of his description – and your name and telephone number. Then if he is brought in I'll give you a ring."

"Thank you," said Jenni. A box on the counter suddenly started rustling.

To Jenni's amazement the receptionist reached in and lifted out a small hedgehog. "Ah, the warmth's woken you up, has it?"

"Shouldn't he be hibernating?" Jenni asked.

"He was," said the receptionist. "Under a bonfire. A boy spotted him and rescued him just before his father lit it. But this little chap's actually too small to go right through the winter. They need to be quite big to be able to survive a whole winter's hibernation. So we'll keep him warm and feed him up."

Jenni stroked the tiny head. "You don't just take cats and dogs then?"

"No. We've got a wildlife wing. We've got rabbits, badgers, all sorts of birds including owls and several foxes."

"I saw a fox this morning," said Jenni. "I didn't know you got wildlife in towns."

"Oh yes, you just have to look a bit harder for it," said the receptionist.

Jenni had an idea. "I was wondering – after I've found my cat – do you need any helpers here? I love helping with animals."

"I'm afraid you're too young yet," said the receptionist. "Hey, don't look so disappointed – in a couple of years we'll be glad of your help." She handed Jenni a piece of paper. "This is a list of things we always need here – things like newspapers and old towels for the animals' cages and runs. Perhaps you could get your mother to save some for us."

"Oh yes," said Jenni. "And I'll bring them in."

"And don't give up hope for your cat," she told Jenni. "It's early days yet."

"I won't," said Jenni. "I'm going to keep searching for him until I find him – no matter how long it takes."

Chapter 5

Puss Makes a Friend

Puss left the railway embankment – and the tree that he'd seen from the alley' way. "That's definitely not my territory."

He put his ears back and scampered off, as yet another train thundered past behind him. "What a racket!" He was amazed the noise hadn't bothered the badger he'd just met. It actually lived in its sett, right there, on the banking.

A few streets further on, Puss spotted more trees in the distance. He instantly cheered up. "That's it. That's bound to be my territory."

The dingy street opened out to a grassy area – but it wasn't what Puss was expecting – it was wasteland. There were a couple of trees, and plenty of grass, but there was also brick rubble lying around and the remains of a building.

"Rabbits!" Puss watched them scampering around and eating the grass. He liked rabbits. Back at home there was a white one called Arabella living next door. He loved to sleep on top of her hutch.

Suddenly all the rabbits disappeared down their holes.

A loud barking from behind told Puss why. He jumped round to see a large black dog racing towards him.

"Ye-owl!" He wasn't keen on dogs at the best of times. And this one was ENORMOUS. Puss – the fearless cat –

pulled himself up on fully stretched legs
and arched his back to make himself look
bigger. He hissed and spat as he gave the
dog his Special Stare. Then he lashed out
with his paw as an extra warning to leave
him alone.

The dog hesitated. But then it lunged
forward with its HUGE red mouth wide
open. There was only one thing to do in
this situation. The not-quite-so-fearless-
cat now turned tail and fled into the ruined
building. But the dog followed.

Puss ran out again. The dog followed.

Puss raced round the bricks. The dog
followed.

He couldn't outrun this dog. He spotted
a small gap in a wall. His sharp senses
immediately told him he could get in but
the dog couldn't. He dived through it

but a sharp piece of brick tore at his fur. "Ouch!"

There was a thud as the dog crashed into the wall. "Stupid dog," said Puss. "Fancy trying to get through that hole. A cat wouldn't make that mistake."

"Butch! What are you doing now?" A man's voice came from outside.

Through the hole in the wall Puss gleefully watched the dog stagger towards its master. It was obviously dizzy from the bump on its head.

The man spotted Puss and gave a laugh. "Well, Butch, I see you've met your match this time. Perhaps this will teach you not to chase cats." He made a quick inspection of the dog to make sure he wasn't injured, then he put his lead on and tied him up to a dead tree stump.

Butch made an instant recovery and started barking.

The man bent down to Puss. "Come on out, Puss," he coaxed. "Let's see if you're all right."

"He called me Puss. I don't know him, but he seems to know me – perhaps he'll take me back to my territory." Puss ventured out of the hole.

He even allowed the man to pick him up. "That's good," said the man as he looked at him. "Apart from a bit of missing fur, you're not injured." He brushed the brick dust off him. "There you are, that's better."

Puss stared down at the dog from the safety of the man's arms. It was barking furiously now – obviously jealous. He rubbed his head under the man's chin and grinned to himself as his actions made the dog bark even more.

"You're a lovely puss, aren't you?" said the man, stroking him. "But where have you come from? I've never seen you round here. I know all the cats." He looked down as Butch gave a frustrated whine. "So does Butch."

Puss was disappointed. He didn't know him after all.

"Are you lost?" the man asked him. "I can't take you home with me, because of Butch. But I could take you to the animal shelter. At least you'd be warm and fed, shut up in there."

Puss had heard enough. "He's not shutting me up anywhere." He leapt out of the man's arms and raced across the grass. "If I'm shut up somewhere I'll never find

Jenni," he panted. What was he thinking about, find Jenni? "I'm looking for my old territory," he corrected himself. "I'm not going back to that DREADFUL house, even if Jenni is there."

Puss found himself on the canal bank. He spotted a bridge and raced across it. Butch and the man – thank goodness – didn't follow him.

He was in a big yard. A crane was loading planks of wood on to a barge on the canal. Puss scampered round the back of some piles of wood.

A movement caught his eye. His senses were alert immediately. It was a mouse! A FREE mouse. He hadn't caught a mouse for AGES.

Puss automatically sprang into action, crouching low and silently, stealthily moving forward. He'd lost none of his skill. A quick, excited wiggle of his bottom and he pounced!

The mouse didn't stand a chance against the fearless hunter.

A white cat suddenly appeared round a pile of wood and Puss was quick to safeguard his catch. He arched his back, his fur standing on end, and hissed at the intruder. "Ssss-stay away. Keep back. This is my catch."

The cat was holding a piece of bread in her mouth and she dropped it in front of him. "I don't want your mouse. I've caught three already this morning."

Puss relaxed a bit. "Three?"

The mouse took advantage as Puss loosened his grip. It made a break for freedom and scampered off into a woodpile.

The first mouse he'd caught in ages – and this silly town cat had made him lose it.

"There are hundreds more round here," said the white cat. "I'll catch one for you if you like."

"No." The fearless hunter certainly didn't need another cat to catch a mouse for him. "I can easily catch one myself – that one was a bit small anyway. Did you say there were . . . hundreds . . . round here?"

The cat nodded. "And the men often give me titbits." She pushed the piece of bread towards him with her paw. "Jim just gave me this – he always shares his lunch with me. Would you like it?"

Puss's nose twitched. It was a piece of cheese sandwich. He chewed on it hungrily. He was getting to quite like cheese sandwiches.

The white cat purred and rubbed herself against him. "Why don't you stay here with me? We could have some fun together."

Chapter 6

It's Puss's Fur!

First thing the next morning Jenni went out to buy a street map of East Deeming. She wanted to put some order into her search, make sure she didn't miss anywhere.

The pigeon was waiting for her when she got back. And it had brought two of its friends with it.

Her mother laughed. "It didn't take you long to find something to feed."

Most of the neighbours had been friendly when Jenni and her father had knocked on their doors last night. They'd agreed to search their gardens and sheds for Puss. Only one old man was grumpy. He told them he hated cats as they dug up his garden.

Mrs Armstrong from number eight told her that her own cat had been hit by a car last month. But it had managed to get home and she had found it hidden in a pile of leaves in the garden. "They often hide away if they're injured," she told Jenni.

Jenni couldn't bear to think of Puss being hurt. But he wasn't used to these dangerous roads. She had to find him soon!

Jenni studied the map for places Puss might have gone to. "There's somewhere I should try." It was an alley-way behind the houses in the next road.

"Puss. Puss." Jenni walked along the alley-way, stopping nervously to examine every pile of dead leaves. She looked into the gardens on either side.

A lady putting food on a bird table looked up as she heard Jenni call Puss. "You must be the little girl who's lost her cat – I saw your poster. He's all black with four white feet, isn't he?"

Jenni nodded. "I call him Puss in Boots."

"What a coincidence," the lady chuckled. "That's the pantomime they're putting on over in Manningford this year. Have you seen the advertisements for it?"

"Yes," said Jenni. "Mum said that perhaps my Puss has gone to seek my fortune – like the one in the pantomime did for his master. But she was just trying to cheer me up."

"I'm sure he'll turn up soon." The lady asked Jenni her name and introduced herself as Mrs Baxter.

Jenni liked her. "Do you get many birds round here? I've only seen pigeons so far and a couple of starlings."

"Oh yes," said Mrs Baxter. "A lot come into the towns in winter. It's warmer you see – all the buildings give a bit of shelter."

"And people like you feed them," said Jenni.

"Yes, I put out wild bird food and scraps like cheese and bread. That's for birds like sparrows, starlings, blackbirds and robins," said Mrs Baxter. "Peanuts and bacon rind attract blue tits, great tits and greenfinches. Oh, and squirrels."

"You get squirrels in the garden?"

"A couple of them. Cheeky little things. But they're hungry too so I don't mind them having some of the peanuts."

"I like squirrels," said Jenny. "And birds. I like all animals really."

A little girl with long blonde hair popped her head over the fence. "I like animals too. D'you want to see my rabbit?"

Jenni went into her garden. She was called Alice and was a couple of years younger than Jenni. Jenni admired Alice's fluffy black and white rabbit. She told her how she'd just moved from the country with her family and that Puss had gone missing.

"I saw something in a pile of leaves just now," said Alice. "Over there. It was moving so I was afraid to look."

Jenni's heart raced as she bent over the pile. It was moving, slowly, almost as if the heap was breathing. Her hands shook as she parted the leaves.

"Ouch!" She pulled her hands away quickly. Something had pricked her. "It's not Puss," she told Alice. "But I think I know what it is." She carefully scraped more leaves away to reveal a large hedgehog curled tightly in a ball.

"Oh, lovely." Alice clapped her hands. "Is he all right?"

"Yes he's fine. He's hibernating," Jenni explained, as she covered him up again. "He's nice and big so he'll be all right to sleep right through the winter."

Alice looked impressed. "I suppose you know that because you used to live in the country."

Jenni smiled. "No, actually I learnt that yesterday. Here, in the town."

"Will you come and see me again?" Alice asked.

Jenni smiled. "Of course I will."

After lunch Jenni decided to search by the canal. It wasn't far according to the map and it was the only bit of open space nearby. Puss was used to open spaces.

Her mother came with her. "It might be nice by the canal," she said.

"I doubt it," said Jenni. "This is a canal – in a town. Not a lovely river like we had in the country. It's probably filthy and full of rubbish."

She was in for a surprise though. The water was clean and clear and there were ducks, geese and swans swimming on it.

Jenni smiled. "I'll bring some bread the next time we come."

They watched a long colourful narrowboat going past and a barge being loaded up outside a wood yard on the opposite bank. The towpath on their side was edged with grass and bushes. A small group of people were cutting back some overgrown trees.

They went to ask them if they'd seen Puss.

"No, sorry," said a young man. "We've only just got here. We'll keep a look out though."

There were a girl and a boy who looked a little older than Jenni and they smiled at her. She smiled shyly back. "What are you doing?"

"We're members of CWAG," said the boy.

"That stands for Canal and Wasteland Action Group," added the girl. "Lots more of us come at the weekends. The group has cleared the canal of rubbish and made it usable again."

"But it's taken a long time," said a lady. "Several years. And we're always looking for more volunteers. There's loads more to do."

Jenni's mum looked interested. "What a wonderful idea. We'd love to help, wouldn't we Jenni?"

The girl smiled at Jenni. "Yes, why don't you join us?"

Jenni smiled back. "I'd love to. But I've got to find my cat first."

The young man gave them a leaflet about the group. Then he suggested they try searching on the adjoining wasteland.

Jenni went there straight away. She ran amongst the bricks and rubble. "Puss. Puss. Are you here?"

She was amazed to see three wild rabbits scampering round the remains of a building. She ran after them, but they had disappeared.

Then she caught sight of something in a hole in the wall.

"It's black fur," she cried, pouncing on it. "Here, caught on this brick. It's Puss's fur."

"Don't get your hopes up too much," warned her mother. "It could be from anything."

"It is Puss's fur," cried Jenni. "I know it is. He's here. Or at least he was here. He can't be far away."

Chapter 7

Spaghetti Bolognese

Puss had been walking for two days. He didn't know where he was. He could have been walking round in circles for all he knew. And he was starving!

"I should have stayed with that friendly white cat," he grumbled to himself. "There was plenty of food – and it was quite nice there." He put his ears back as he set off again. "But it wasn't home. And I'll never find my territory if I don't keep looking. Fearless cats don't give up that easily."

He'd found a few titbits on a rubbish

dump, which he'd shared with a family of foxes and about two hundred screaming seagulls. But that had been yesterday morning.

Then he smelt it. A really delicious meaty smell. His mouth began to water. The smell was coming from behind a sort of shop. "Perhaps there's a nice old lady there like the one who used to give me titbits back at home,"

The smell got stronger as he made his way down the side driveway to the back. There was a delivery van parked there and a lot of shouting coming from the shop. Puss cautiously peered round to see what was happening.

A man in a tall white hat was doing the shouting. "I've-a been waiting for this spaghetti for over an hour." He was very red in the face. 'I'm-a famous chef, you know. The customers love-a my delicious, out-of-this-world, home-made Spaghetti Bolognese."

"I'm sorry," said the other man. "I couldn't find your restaurant."

The chef followed him out to the van. "All-a the meat is cooked and waiting. But Spaghetti Bolognese I cannot make-a without spaghetti."

Puss put his head on one side. He could see the cooked meat on a worktop just inside the door. He sniffed the air and breathed in the delicious smell. The kitchen was empty. "Surely he won't miss a little bit of it."

The chef was still shouting at the man as they looked in the back of the van. "Now's my chance." As quick as a flash

Puss was inside the kitchen and on to the worktop. He gulped down two mouthfuls of the warm Bolognese sauce. The chef was right – it was delicious.

A scream made him drop his next mouthful. The chef's face, in the doorway, had turned almost purple now. He was spluttering and spitting as though he couldn't get his words out.

Puss leapt down and cowered in a corner as the chef threw a ladle at him. "You-a vile animal. You-a hateful, flea-ridden, filthy bit of vermin. How-a can I give that to people now?"

Puss shrank back as a saucepan lid came towards him. He didn't see why he couldn't give the meat to people. It had tasted all right to him – and he'd only eaten a little bit.

The chef advanced towards him with a HUGE saucepan in his hand. Puss had seen enough. He shot through the chefs legs and skidded out of the door. The saucepan clattered down behind him as he raced round the side of the restaurant.

"I'll-a get you for this," screamed the chef after him. "I'll-a search for you till I find you. I'll-a make you sorry."

Puss didn't stop running for a long time. Then he sat down to get his breath back and to have a good wash. "What a fuss," he said, as he licked his right foot and rubbed it over his right ear. "I only had two mouthfuls. There was plenty left." He carefully licked all along the black fur on his back. "How dare he call me vermin. And especially FLEA-RIDDEN and FILTHY. I've got a beautiful coat – Jenni says so."

He felt a twinge of sadness as he thought of leaving Jenni behind. She'd probably miss him. And she'd miss the mice he used to bring in for her. The look on her face when she saw them made all his efforts worthwhile. She had such fun chasing them all over the house.

He quickly shook himself. He had to get on. He finished cleaning each of his white boots and set off again.

He walked and walked. He crossed another canal – or was it the same canal but a different bridge? This place was so confusing. One time he thought he recognized a very tall building but then he wasn't sure.

"I can't be losing my touch. Does hunger make you confused?"

Puss spent the night in an alley-way

behind some houses. He curled up in a pile of leaves under a bush. At least it was away from the traffic.

A small terrier dog woke him up in the morning. She yapped at him through her gate. "Come and play. Come and play," she called. "I've got a ball. I've got a ball."

She looked friendly enough – even though she was a dog – but Puss couldn't stop to play. He had to get on with finding his territory. "I bet Ginger Tom is having a good laugh about taking it over."

He jumped up on to the wall of the next garden to see if he could spot anything familiar – or even something to eat. "What's that?" It was a rabbit in a hutch. But Puss saw immediately it wasn't Arabella. This one was black and white and a little girl with long blonde hair was talking to it.

He ran along the wall to the next garden and lots of birds flew off. Jenni didn't allow him to chase birds.

"Why do I keep thinking about Jenni?"

Puss sniffed the air. "Bacon. And cheese." He looked over to a bird table. Jenni often put bits of food out for the birds. He'd never bothered about it before – never lowered himself to eat the birds' scraps. "But I've never been this hungry – and there might even be a cheese sandwich."

He jumped down and started to make his way across the grass. Then the back door opened and a lady came out. She gave a gasp as she spotted him. "Well, my-oh-my. Fancy seeing you here."

Puss hesitated. He was sure he didn't know her.

"Come on then," she coaxed. "Come here, boy."

Puss took a step towards her. She looked nice and there was a smell of cooking coming from the house.

"Good boy," she said. "Come on. There's someone looking for you. Been searching everywhere, they have."

"Ye-owl!" Puss stopped immediately. The mad chef had people out looking for him. He turned tail and ran. Out of the garden. Down the alley-way. Down the next street, over a fence and out on to the road.

There was a deafening squeal of brakes as a car skidded towards him.

Chapter 8

Poor Little Cat

Jenni studied the map. Puss hadn't been on the wasteland or along the canal – or anywhere else in the surrounding area. She'd been back again and again.

There was a knock at the front door and she heard her father go to answer it. It was Sunday and he'd promised to spend the morning helping her search.

"Perhaps it's someone with news of Puss." They were getting to know quite a few of the neighbours now. They often asked after Puss and even stopped for a chat. Mum said it sometimes took an animal to get people talking.

"Jenni."

Jenni looked up to see Mrs Baxter, who had been feeding the birds yesterday. She was out of breath and looked excited. "I've seen him – Puss in Boots. All black with four white feet. In my garden – ten minutes ago."

Jenni jumped up. "Oh, thank goodness. Where is he? Did you catch him?"

"I'm sorry, but he ran away from me."

Jenni jumped up and grabbed her coat. "Was he all right?"

"He looked fine," said Mrs Baxter. "Come on, I'll help you find him."

Jenni's father joined them and they raced round to Mrs Baxter's garden.

They searched up and down the alley and

in all the gardens. Alice and her mother came out to help and so did a lady with a small terrier dog. They looked round all the surrounding streets – but there was no sign of him.

Jenni didn't want to go back for dinner but her father insisted. She was upset and frustrated. "He can't have got far. Oh, why did he run off again?"

After dinner Mum and Dad were going to the canal to join the members of CWAG. "Your father's already phoned to say we'll be there," said Mum. "So we've got to go. And at least you know Puss is okay now. He can't be far away. Why don't you come with us? You've been searching non-stop for five days."

"No," said Jenni. "I've got to keep looking for him."

As soon as they'd left Jenni put on her yellow and black trainers. She smiled as she looked at the tiger's face on the toe. Puss had been so funny the first time he'd seen them, pouncing on them then jumping back and pouncing again. She was going to thoroughly search the whole area again – he was somewhere nearby. He couldn't have gone far – she was bound to find him this afternoon.

Then the phone rang. "I've just seen a black and white cat," said the voice on the other end. "It was knocked down by a car in Market Street, I'm afraid. I think it might be dead."

"Oh no!" Jenni uttered a garbled "Thank you" and put the phone down. She grabbed her coat and flew out of the door. She knew the area so well now she knew exactly where Market Street was.

It was only two roads away but it seemed miles as she raced round there. She felt sick with worry and guilt. "I shouldn't have gone home for dinner. I should have stayed out looking – I bet he was knocked down while I was actually eating."

She turned the corner into Market Street. "Oh, please, please let him be all right."

Her eyes immediately focused on a small black and white body lying in the gutter. "Oh no!" She raced towards it. He was so still – he looked. . . She couldn't bring herself to even think the word.

She dropped down on her hands and knees. She was shaking badly as her eyes rapidly took in the black and white fur.

It wasn't Puss.

"Oh, thank goodness." Jenni was still shaking, but an immense feeling of relief flooded over her. Puss wasn't dead. He was still missing – but he wasn't dead.

"Poor little cat," she whispered to the tiny bundle in the gutter.

She heard footsteps running towards her and stood up to see a boy of around her age.

"Saskia!" he cried. He turned to Jenni, his eyes wide with pain. "That's my cat."

"Oh, I'm so sorry." Jenni felt terrible as she looked at him. She'd been so relieved it wasn't Puss – but of course it had to be someone's cat.

The boy was obviously trying hard not to cry. "I don't know what to do. Mum and Dad are out."

Jenni felt so sorry for him. She reached out and put her arms round him to give him a hug. "What's your name?"

"Mark."

Over Mark's shoulder she blinked back the tears herself as she looked down at the poor little cat.

It twitched!

It twitched again.

"She's not dead!" she cried.

Mark appeared to be frozen to the spot so Jenni took charge. "Where's the nearest vet?" she asked, tearing off her coat.

"In the next road," said Mark. "What are you doing?"

"Help me," said Jenni, laying her coat out on the pavement. Together they carefully lifted Saskia on to the coat and Jenni wrapped her up in it to keep her warm.

Mark had pulled himself together and led the way as they ran round to the vet's. All the way Jenni was willing the little bundle in her arms to hang on – to stay alive.

The vet was called Miss Williams and she immediately connected Saskia to a drip. "It's to counteract the shock," she explained, as she covered the little cat up to keep her warm. "The first thing is to get her over the shock and then we can find out what injuries she has and treat them."

They had to leave her there. Miss Williams said it was just a matter of waiting to see if she came round.

Jenni walked back with Mark to his house. He wanted to wait in, in case the vet phoned. "Thanks, Jenni," he said. "Thanks a lot for your help."

Jenni gave him her phone number. "Please let me know how Saskia gets on.

I've got to go now as my own cat's missing and I've got to keep searching for him."

"Oh, I'm sorry," said Mark. "Have you tried looking over the council rubbish dump? Or the wasteland?"

"I've tried everywhere," said Jenni. "But I'm trying it all again and again. I've got this strange feeling that I keep on just missing him."

Chapter 9

Missing Jenni

Puss was really fed up. He'd walked miles and miles and there was no sign of his old territory. But to his surprise he found he wasn't so bothered about that now. He was missing Jenni. Oh, how he was missing Jenni. And he didn't know how to find her again.

He stood and watched the traffic. He was learning to be more careful – a car had only just missed him the other day when he ran into the road. And yesterday he had heard some people talking about a cat that had actually been hit by a car. In somewhere called Market Street. He didn't know if it was dead or not but apparently a boy and a girl had taken it to see Vet.

"Wait a minute." He had a sudden thought. "If Vet is nearby maybe I can find him. Although I was always taken there in the car. . . But then I was brought here in the car too. It seemed a bit longer getting here – but it must be the same place."

He pictured the large man in his white coat as he set off along the pavement again. "He should be easy enough to recognize. And he's bound to remember me – he said he'd never forget me after my last visit. Well, who could blame me for wrecking his surgery? The embarrassment of it!"

He gave an indignant twitch of his tail as he remembered something called a thermometer. He hadn't known where to look when Vet had stuck it into his bottom!

"One or two broken bottles and a few scratches were nothing to the embarrassment I suffered. It was all right for Vet telling me it was the usual way to take an animal's temperature. It wasn't him standing there with a thermometer stuck in his bottom." Puss paused. Did he actually want to see Vet again?

"Yes," he decided, setting off. "When Vet sees me he'll phone Jenni and she'll come and get me."

Puss stopped for a rest. He'd walked along countless streets. Past houses and shops, over bridges, under bridges, in and out of alley-ways. But there was no sign of Vet.

"It's a wonder I haven't worn my feet out, walking on all this hard ground," he said. "I'm sure my legs are getting shorter."

He was so tired and so hungry. He was beginning to feel weak from lack of food – and he'd had a fight with a big black tom-cat. And he'd lost! The fearless cat had never lost a fight in his life before.

"Of course he was EXCEPTIONALLY big," said Puss. "And he had obviously had an ENORMOUS dinner – so I didn't stand a chance." He sat down to lick his sore leg where the big bully had bitten him.

"I can't think why he was so aggressive – that tiny square of grass he called HIS garden was hardly worth defending."

He stood up as a group of youngsters came towards him. Perhaps Jenni was with them. They stopped right next to him and he quickly looked up at all the faces.

She wasn't there.

"Have you seen Puss?" one of them asked.

Puss's heart jumped. They must be friends of Jenni's. They were looking for him. He immediately ran forward, his tail held erect. "Miaow. I'm here."

They didn't hear him. The trouble is, my deep, throaty, masculine cry is a bit weak these days, he thought.

"I think he's going to meet us there," said a boy.

"Where?" Puss panicked as the group moved off chattering excitedly. "Where's THERE? Where am I supposed to meet them? And will Jenni be THERE too?"

He'd have to follow them. He limped

after them, through a huge gateway and into a sort of field with grass and trees. But cars were driving through it and there were strange creatures in the distance with huge antlers on their heads.

"Funny looking cows," said Puss.

It seemed a long way and Puss was exhausted. Only the thought of finding Jenni again kept him going.

They eventually stopped outside a hall.

"There he is," said a girl. "There's Puss."

"At last!" Puss looked up expectantly. But the girl was pointing at a boy. A SILLY boy with big boots on and whiskers drawn on his face. "Come on," said the boy. "The pantomime's due to start in an hour."

Puss didn't know what they were talking about. But he did know it wasn't him they were looking for. And Jenni wasn't there either.

He was tired, weak and very, very hungry. There was a cardboard box next to the hall door and he dejectedly crawled inside. Somehow, the fearless cat – the fearless hunter – just didn't feel fearless any more.

It started to snow. Puss remembered snow – he usually liked to play in it. But not this time.

He curled up in the box to keep warm and watched the snowflakes falling thickly outside. "I'd have been better off staying at THAT house," he murmured. "At least I would have been warm and fed. And I'd have been with Jenni. . ."

Chapter 10

Jenni's Treat

"It's starting to snow," Jenni's mother called to her. "We're going to have a white Christmas."

Jenni looked out of the window. She remembered Puss in the snow last year. He was so funny, jumping up and down in it and trying to bite it. She thought about him all the time.

The brightly decorated Christmas tree made her think of him trying to climb it when he was a kitten. And of him jumping up to catch the silver and gold baubles.

He'd actually knocked the tree right over one year.

Wrapping her presents for Mum and Dad reminded her how he loved chasing the ribbon as she tried to tie it. Jenni didn't want any presents this year – all she wanted was Puss.

"Christmas Eve," she sighed. "And still no sign of him. This is my worst Christmas ever." Jenni put her trainers on again – they'd be good for gripping on the snow. She tried hard to keep her spirits up but it was getting harder and harder as the days went by.

"You're not going out again in all that snow, are you?" asked her mother. "You've been out all morning and you've only been in for ten minutes to eat your lunch."

"I've got to keep searching," said Jenni.

She opened the front door and threw some bread to about fourteen pigeons waiting on the paving slabs. A couple of sparrows had joined them today. "And I'll be going out again tomorrow – Christmas Day. I won't give up."

"I'm just a bit worried about you. You're not getting any rest," said her mother. "I'll help again later, when I've finished icing the Christmas cake." The phone rang and she went to answer it.

Jenni waited. It might be about Puss. So many people were concerned about him now. Every time Jenni went out someone stopped her to ask if there was any news. People were so much friendlier round here than she'd first thought.

And the area didn't seem so bad now she was getting used to it. She'd seen several more foxes, and a couple of squirrels searching for their winter store of nuts. Even a badger when Dad took her to the railway embankment one evening.

Dad was making her a bird table and they were going to have a pond. Mr Samuels from number twenty-four had told them that garden ponds in towns provided essential breeding sites for frogs and toads. There were fewer sites in the countryside now as ponds and ditches were filled in. And hedgehogs were finding more food available in people's gardens – more and more wildlife was adapting to living in towns.

The canal area was nice and the wasteland would be nice too when the members of CWAG had converted it into a nature park. But without Puss she couldn't appreciate anything.

"Jenni. Wait a minute." Her mother called from the phone.

Jenni's heart leapt. "Is it about Puss?" Perhaps it was the animal shelter to say he was there, safe and sound. But she'd already been there this morning to drop off some newspapers and he hadn't been there then.

"No. It's Mark, for you. I've just been chatting to his mum."

Jenni rushed to the phone. "It'll be about Saskia."

"She's going to be okay," cried Mark. "Saskia's broken a back leg and she's got bruising to her lower back – but she's going to recover. We've just brought her home."

"Oh, I'm so pleased she's all right," said Jenni.

"Well, it's mainly thanks to you. Miss

Williams said if you hadn't acted so quickly Saskia would probably have died of shock," Mark told her. "Mum wants to give you a treat to say thank you. Can you come round?"

"Oh, I don't know. . ." said Jenni. She looked up at her mother.

"Mark's mum has already asked me if it's okay," said her mother. "You go. You deserve a treat. And you need a break. Dad will be home early today and then we'll both go out and look for Puss for you."

"All right," Jenni agreed. "Thank you," she said to Mark down the phone. "I would like to come and see Saskia."

Saskia was a lovely cat. Her markings were quite different to Jenni's Puss with his boots. Saskia was black with white on her face and throat and two white legs and feet. And one pink leg – that was the broken one in plaster.

Mark was the same age as Jenni and was very nice. "I'll help you search for your cat after Christmas," he told her.

His mother was nice too. She was taking them out, but she wouldn't tell Jenni where – it was a surprise. Jenni would much rather have carried on looking for Puss but Mark and his mother were being so kind to her. She'd have to try and enjoy herself for their sake. And she was pleased to have made a friend.

They were going by car, as it was quite a long way. The windscreen wipers swished away the snowflakes that were falling steadily now.

"We're going through the park," said

Mark. "Have you been there? It's just into Manningford – it's very nice."

"No I haven't been out of East Deeming," said Jenni. "I've been too busy searching for my cat."

She looked out of the window as they drove through the park. It did look nice. There was a lake and she saw a herd of fallow deer in the distance. At the moment it looked rather like a scene on a Christmas card with all the snow on the bare branches of the trees.

They drove out of the park on the other side and pulled up outside a hall.

"We're here," cried Mark. "I'm really looking forward to this."

As they walked towards the gate, Jenni looked up at the big colourful banner above the door. It read:

THREE O'CLOCK TODAY
CHRISTMAS PANTOMIME
PUSS IN BOOTS

Oh no." Jenni stopped and stared at it in horror. This was to be her treat. To watch *Puss in Boots*! Tears welled up in her eyes. She couldn't sit and watch it –not with her own Puss in Boots missing.

"What's the matter?" asked Mark.

"My cat – the one that's missing. I – I didn't get a chance to tell you before –but I call him Puss in Boots."

"Oh no," said Mark. "I'm so sorry – I didn't know."

His mother put her arm round Jenni. "Would you like me to take you home again, dear?"

Jenni nodded. Then she looked at her watch. "But it's three o'clock – the pantomime's just starting. If you take me back now, you and Mark will miss it too."

Chapter 11

The Best Christmas Ever

Puss shifted in his cardboard box. Something had woken him, disturbed him. People had been going past for ages. But this was different – it was something familiar.

"The voice. It's Jenni's voice!" He uncurled himself and peered out of his box. "Miaow. Jenni, I'm here."

Where was she? She couldn't have heard him. If only his voice wasn't so weak now.

He crawled stiffly out of the box. A group

of people were just coming up the path but she wasn't with them.

Then his sharp hearing picked out Jenni's voice again. "I can't make you miss the pantomime – it wouldn't be fair. Mark just said he was looking forward to it," she was saying. "I will come in. I – I expect I'll be all right."

Puss's sensitive ears immediately located the direction – Jenni was just behind these people.

He shot off down the slippery path. As he skidded towards the group, he caught a glimpse of Jenni through their legs. "She's there – down by the gate!" He frantically tried to dodge round the hurrying feet but he slipped on the trodden snow. Then a HUGE boot kicked him.

"Ye-owl!" Puss was knocked off his

paws. He rolled over and over down a bank until he came to a halt up against a bush.

He scrambled to his feet again and shook himself. "I've got to get to Jenni."

But the huge boots had followed him. "Are you all right?" A man picked him up and began brushing the snow off him. "I hope I didn't hurt you."

Puss couldn't wait around to be comforted. He had to get to Jenni. So he did the only thing he could – he bit the man's hand to make him let go.

Once free, he clawed his way back up the bank, gripping on the grass beneath the snow. The rest of the people had gone now and he raced down the path. He skidded to a halt at the gate.

Jenni had disappeared. "Where is she?"

Puss spun round and saw her. She was at the top of the path now – almost up to his box.

He raced back up the slippery path. "Miaow. Jenni! Miaow."

Puss reached the top just as Jenni disappeared into the hall.

Suddenly there was a big burst of music and people were clapping. Puss hesitated and put his ears back. "What a noise." But he had to go in there. "I've got to get to Jenni."

"Hey!" shouted a lady as Puss squeezed through her legs.

It was a huge place – so noisy and so many people. Where was Je—?

"Ye-owl!" Puss was suddenly swung into the air as the lady grabbed him by the scruff of his neck.

Then he was outside again.

"Sorry, we don't allow cats in here," said the lady, and laughed. "At least, not real ones."

Puss yowled and wriggled and squirmed in her grip. The man with huge boots appeared in the doorway. "I think that cat's wild," he said, as he went into the hall.

Puss was dropped down into the snow. Too true he was wild. And furious. He immediately scrabbled round again to get back in. But the lady was too quick for him. She closed the door in his face.

He scratched and scratched at the door until his claws hurt. But no one let him in. They probably couldn't hear him anyway with all that music and clapping and shouting. "What on earth's going on in there?"

He crawled back into his box. "I'll just have to wait for Jenni to come out again. She's got to come out sometime."

Puss settled down to clean off his fur with one eye firmly fixed on the door. He was tired, hungry – and completely exhausted. His side hurt from the kick and he ached all over. But he couldn't go to sleep. "I mustn't miss Jenni coming out."

Puss fought hard to stay awake but his eyelids kept drooping. "Why doesn't Jenni come out? What's she doing in there?" His head nodded forward.

Puss was jolted awake as laughing, chattering people streamed out of the hall. But all he could see was a flurry of boots and shoes kicking up the freshly fallen snow. He panicked. "I'll never find Jenni in all this. Why have so many people come out at the same time?"

Had he missed her already? He joined in amongst the mass of legs moving down the path towards the gate. He couldn't see past them and he certainly couldn't see up to any faces.

Then, ahead of him, through a small gap, he spotted something familiar. Yellow and black trainers with a tiger's face on them. "Jenni's shoes!" But she was way ahead of him – she must be almost at the gate.

"Miaow. Jenni! Miaow." She couldn't hear him. "I've got to get to her. If she goes without me, I might never find her again."

Puss desperately tried to push his way through the mass of legs.

"What's going on?" said a lady.

"It's a wild cat," said Huge Boots. "Watch your ankles – he bites."

Puss got past him as he stood aside. Then he managed to push past several more people. They were all moving so slowly – but at least that meant he wasn't so likely to be kicked. If only he could get through. . .

He squeezed between a boy's legs. Then, at last, he was at the gate.

But Jenni had gone. "Where is she?" Puss frantically looked around him.

"Oh no. She's in that car. She's leaving."

Somehow, Puss gathered together every last bit of strength he had left. He raced forward and jumped up on to the bonnet just as the car started to move off. His claws screeched on the slippery paintwork as he fought to steady himself.

The lady in the driving seat screamed. The car shuddered to a halt.

Then the doors were flung open and Jenni was there. "Puss!" she shrieked. She was laughing and crying at the same time as she picked him up. "Oh where have you been? And look at you, you're so thin."

Puss snuggled into her. His side hurt where Jenni was squeezing him but he didn't care. He was with Jenni again – his Jenni.

A boy was jumping up and down on the pavement. And the lady was saying something about getting them home.

Then they all got into the car. Puss purred and purred as he settled down on Jenni's lap. She was as soft as he remembered and she smelt so nice. She was stroking him and kissing him on his head. "Oh, I've missed you so much," she said. "I do love you, Puss."

Puss usually got embarrassed with all that sort of thing – but today he didn't care.

"I can't believe I've found you at last," said Jenni, tickling him behind his ears – just the way he liked it. "Although it was really you who found me. But whatever are you doing here? It's such a long way from home. However did you get here?"

Puss pushed his head under her chin and thought to himself that it was something to do with a mad chef chasing him. And a silly boy with big boots on and whiskers drawn on his face.

"You know what?" Jenni started to laugh. "The Puss in the pantomime went off and found riches and good fortune for his master. And in a different sort of way that's just what you did for me. Through searching for you I've met friends and neighbours – and I've realized it's not so bad round here after all. And there's lots to do."

"And don't forget about Saskia," said Mark. "If you hadn't been searching for Puss you wouldn't have found my cat and helped me with her."

"No," Jenni agreed. "This is Mark, Puss. He's my friend. You'll like his cat – she's called Saskia."

Mark grinned at Puss. "You're a fearless little cat, aren't you? Jumping up on a moving car like that."

Puss snuggled into Jenni's lap. The boy was obviously intelligent – he'd realized straight away what a fearless cat he was. The woman looked okay too. And anyway, he'd just made a decision. From now on anywhere Jenni wanted to be was okay with him.

"And there's a nice rabbit that lives just round the corner," Jenni told him. "You like rabbits, don't you? This one belongs to Alice – you'll like her too. Then there's a friendly lady who feeds the birds. . ."

Puss closed his eyes as Jenni talked softly to him – and purred even louder. He was actually looking forward to going back to his new home. To being in the warm and to lots of good food. And at least he had his own territory there.

All right, so the back garden's a bit small, he thought. But it'll take me less time to defend it – give me more time to spend sleeping.

And as soon as I'm fit again, he decided, I'm going to find that black tom-cat. Sort him out, show him who's boss round here.

Jenni gave him a big cuddle. "You're all I wanted for Christmas. This is the best Christmas ever." She gave him another kiss. "Happy Christmas, Puss in Boots."

The Christmas Pony

Chapter 1

Mr Crumbs

"Of course you can't have a pony for Christmas, Laura. We couldn't possibly afford one." Dad looked determined.

"But it's not just any pony – it's Mr Crumbs," said Laura. "And he's free to a good home."

"Ponies cost a fortune to keep," said Mum. "And apart from that we've got nowhere for him to live."

"We'd find somewhere—"

"No, Laura," said Dad. "You know how difficult things are at the moment."

"But if we can't give him a home he'll have to go and live at the horse and pony sanctuary," said Laura. "We'll never see him."

"I'm sorry, but the answer's still no," said Dad, in his don't-you-argue-with-me voice. "It's just not possible."

He went back out to the garage to finish the oil change on Mr Robert's Volvo and Mum went to answer the telephone.

"Told you they wouldn't agree," said Ben. "It's not practical."

Laura spun round to face her brother. "Oh, why do you always have to be so – so sensible."

"Probably 'cos I'm older than you."

"Only one year," said Laura.

"Dad's been really worried about money since he got made redundant," said Ben.

"Especially as he had to take out that big bank loan to start the business."

"I know, I know – I had noticed," said Laura. Dad was always in his garage these days, repairing cars for people or out doing weddings in his vintage Daimler. And Mum spent most of her time in her workroom, making wedding dresses. "But there must be something we can do."

Laura marched out of the room feeling angry and frustrated. She couldn't just give up. She put on her coat and headed for the front door – a visit to Mr Crumbs always made her feel better.

She set off down the lane and soon spotted Mr Crumbs. He was across the field socializing with the goats on the other side of the fence. He loved company. His sharp hearing immediately picked up Laura's footsteps and he raised his head and gave a loud whinny. With his ears pricked he trotted over to her.

The late November sun shone on his golden coat – it was the colour of toast crumbs, hence his name. Mr Crumbs was a Palomino pony – his pale mane and tail contrasted beautifully with his golden coat. He had a white blaze on his nose and a white stocking on one of his hind legs.

Laura closed the gate behind her and smiled up at the pony.

"Hello, Crumbs." She stroked his warm, broad forehead, but he immediately tried to push his large nose into her pocket, eager to find out if she had something for him.

Laura laughed as he nudged her. "Steady

on. You'll knock me over." She took out the ready-sliced carrot and gave him a piece.

He watched her with his velvet-brown eyes as he crunched on his favourite treat. Then he tilted his head and peered out of the corner of his eye to see if she had any more carrot in her other hand. Ben called that his "quizzical look".

Laura laughed and gave him the second piece. "There's no fooling you, is there!" She loved the feel of his silky-soft muzzle on her hand as he quickly searched out the carrot and gently took it. Mr Crumbs never failed to cheer her up, but this time she couldn't help feeling a little sad.

"I'm afraid Mum and Dad said no," Laura told him, as she patted his firm shoulder. "But don't you worry, I'll think of a way to keep you."

Mr Crumbs tossed his head, shaking his long mane, and blew gently down his nostrils. Laura couldn't imagine life without him. For as long as she could remember he'd been there, in his field. They passed him on their way into town, and on their way to school. At first they'd just stopped to talk to him every day, and sometimes have a chat with Mrs Cox, his owner.

Gradually they'd spent more and more time with him. Then a year ago Mrs Cox had been ill, and Laura and Ben had helped look after Mr Crumbs. When she was better they'd continued to help and in return she'd taught them both to ride him. But now Mrs Cox was moving to Australia to live near her daughter, and a leisure centre was going to be built on her house and land. She had to find a new home for Mr Crumbs before she left.

"Mrs Cox says no one will buy you because you're too old," said Laura. "I don't think you're old – you're only eighteen. You could easily live till you're twenty-five."

She reached up to scratch him between his ears, under his forelock, and Mr Crumbs bent his head towards her. Next to carrots, his favourite thing in life was a good scratch under his forelock.

She heard the gate click and turned to see Ben.

"Hello, Crumbs," said Ben, reaching up to pat him on his glossy neck.

Mr Crumbs greeted him with a soft whinny.

"Mrs Cox says they're very kind at the

horse and pony sanctuary," said Ben. "And he'll have lots of company."

"But it's miles and miles away. We'll never see him," said Laura. "I thought you wanted to keep him too."

"I do." Ben adjusted his glasses with his free hand. "You know I do – but I can understand the reasons why we can't."

Tiggy, Mrs Cox's cat, strolled over to them and Mr Crumbs put his head down to greet her.

"He's going to miss Tiggy – and the goats – as well as Mrs Cox," said Laura. "I can't bear the thought of him missing us too."

She put her arms round Mr Crumbs's neck and hugged him. "I've decided what I'm going to do. I'm going to raise the money to keep him myself."

"How?"

"There are loads of ways."

"Such as?"

"Oh, loads and loads of ways – I'll think of something."

She kissed Mr Crumbs on his soft nose. "I won't let you be sent away to strangers. They won't know where you like to be scratched or what your favourite treats are. I'm going to find a way to keep you – somehow."

Chapter 2

The Mr Crumbs Committee

"Emily says she'll help me raise the money," said Laura. "And she's offered to help look after Mr Crumbs."

"What does Emily know about looking after a pony?" said Mum. "I know she's your best friend, but this isn't a game. It's a big commitment."

"She knows that," said Laura. "She's been with me to visit Mr Crumbs lots of times and she loves him too. I'll teach her how to look after him."

"Emily's mum won't have any money to spare for a pony," said Dad.

"I told you. We're going to raise the money ourselves," said Laura. "Emily's coming round in a minute to discuss it."

"All right. You find out how much it costs to keep a pony," said Dad. "Then, if you can raise enough money in advance to keep Mr Crumbs for at least six months – and find somewhere to keep him – we'll think about it."

Laura was over the moon. Things were looking hopeful. But as her parents left the room she heard Dad whisper to Mum. "She's just a kid," he said. "She'll never do it – not six months' money in advance. We're quite safe."

"How dare he call me 'just a kid'," Laura complained to Ben. "And how dare he say I'll fail before I've even started."

"No, that was unfair," said Ben. "It even made me cross."

"Then why don't you help us?" said Laura. "Let's prove to Dad and Mum that we can do it. We can own Mr Crumbs between the three of us – you, me and Emily."

Ben took his glasses off, polished them on his jumper and put them back on again. "Well, I suppose we could just do a business plan and see if it might work."

"A what?"

"A business plan. Like Dad did when he was setting up the business. It's what all good businesspeople do to see if their ideas are practical."

"But we're not a bus –" Laura started, but quickly stopped herself. Maybe it was a good idea – especially if it meant that Ben would help. . .

As soon as Emily arrived, they all sat down at the kitchen table.

"This is so exciting," said Emily, shaking back her long dark hair. "I can't believe that we might own Mr Crumbs by Christmas."

"Now hold on, don't get too excited," Ben warned her. "It might not be practical. It's a pretty big thing, owning a pony."

"We can do it," said Laura. "I know we can."

"Well, the first thing is to see if it's possible," said Ben. He had just put his calculator on the table and opened his notebook when there was a knock on the back door.

Ben's friend, Sanjay, popped his head round it. "Hiya! You ready to go, Ben?"

Ben jumped up. "Sorry, Laura, I'm off. We're going out on our bikes."

"You can't leave yet," said Laura. "We've only just started."

"Started what?" said Sanjay, shutting the door behind him.

Ben explained about Mr Crumbs.

"Don't you want to keep him then?" asked Sanjay. "I think it would be fantastic to own a pony."

"It's not that I don't want to keep him," said Ben. "I just don't think it will work."

"Well, I'd certainly want to give it a try if it were me," said Sanjay. "I've always fancied having my own pony."

Laura thought quickly. "Would you like to join us, Sanjay? It'd be better with four people – cheaper for all of us."

"Wow! That'd be amazing," said Sanjay, grabbing a seat and drawing it up to the table. "Imagine – owning Mr Crumbs."

"Brilliant!" said Laura. "Let's get started." Another advantage of Sanjay joining them was that there were now three different families involved. If any of them were on holiday – or ill – there would always be someone to look after Mr Crumbs.

"I thought we could call ourselves The Mr Crumbs Committee," said Laura.

"Great," said Emily.

Ben opened his notebook. He wrote THE MR CRUMBS COMMITTEE and listed their names. "We need to work out how much money we think we can raise, and how much it will cost to keep him. And don't forget we haven't got much time. Mrs Cox is moving just after Christmas."

"Christmas is only four-and-a-half weeks away," said Emily.

"Exactly," said Ben.

They started by discussing their pocket money. Laura and Ben got two pounds fifty a week each. Emily got two pounds and Sanjay got four pounds a week, as he helped with recycling all the packaging in his dad's chemist's shop.

After some discussion, they decided it would be fair to put one pound a week each into the fund. They would all need some money to themselves – for Christmas presents, sweets and CDs – and Ben was saving up for a computer.

"Right, fundraising," said Laura. "I thought car-cleaning – we might get some business from Dad's clients."

"Dog-walking," said Sanjay.

"Shopping," said Ben.

"Snow-clearing," said Emily.

They all looked at her. "But it's not snowing."

"It might. If it gets a bit colder," said Emily. "I love snow."

Ben wrote it all down. "We could charge two pounds for everything we do. Keep it simple."

He quickly worked out that if they each did one job a week – for two pounds – and added the one pound from their pocket money, the total between them would be twelve pounds a week.

"That should be plenty – surely," Laura said.

"Well, the next thing is to find out how much it will cost to keep Mr Crumbs," said Ben.

"There's his food," said Laura.

"Vet's bills," said Sanjay.

"Bedding?" said Emily.

"And rent – if we can find somewhere to keep him," said Ben.

"What about the field with Maggie's goats on?" suggested Sanjay.

"That's been bought up for the leisure centre too," said Ben. "Maggie's moving down to Sussex and taking the goats with her."

"We'll soon find somewhere else," said Laura.

Ben listed everything down. "When we've found out all the information we'll be able to see if it will be practical."

Laura smiled to herself. Of course it would be "practical". It was going to work out – she just knew it was.

Chapter 3

Making Plans

Later that afternoon, the four friends met up at Mrs Cox's and Laura gave Emily her first lesson on grooming.

Mr Crumbs loved being groomed. He closed his eyes and gave a low snicker as Laura worked over his neck with the dandy brush.

Laura smiled. "That's his favourite bit."

"He's gorgeous," said Emily, patting his glossy shoulder.

Laura showed her how to brush Mr Crumbs's beautiful mane and tail with the body brush. She brushed each of his legs and then gave him a drink of water.

The pony looked up expectantly as Ben arrived back with his food bucket. He pawed the ground impatiently until it was given to him. Sanjay carried the hay net and the two boys hung it up in the stable.

Mrs Cox arrived with mugs of hot chocolate for them all. "I'm thrilled to bits about your plans to keep Mr Crumbs," she told them. "I do hope it works out. I'll be much happier knowing that I'm leaving him with people he loves – and who love him."

She didn't think it was impossible at all. Laura and Ben had proved how well they could look after Mr Crumbs during the past year. The only thing she insisted on was that they all had their parents' permission and that they found secure premises to keep him in – with supervision from an experienced adult. "However capable I know you are," she said, "I'm afraid I can't just hand Mr Crumbs over to you."

As they sipped their drinks they watched Mr Crumbs munching intently in his large bucket, sorting out the carrots to eat first. Gradually an orange, slobbery mess formed round his mouth.

Laura chuckled. "That's why I leave washing his muzzle until last."

"Good thinking!" said Mrs Cox, laughing. "Now, you asked about the cost of keeping him. I've done a few quick calculations. There's his compound mix, vitamins, hay – oh, and his carrots." She smiled at her pony's orange lips. "We mustn't forget his carrots. So, all his food, and straw for his bedding, adds up to about ten pounds a week."

Ben whipped out his notebook and wrote it down.

"Then there's his shoes."

Laura sighed. They'd forgotten about shoes. It was already going to cost more than she'd thought.

"Mr Norris comes every six to eight weeks and does them for me for forty-five pounds," said Mrs Cox.

"Forty-five pounds?" said Emily. "Every six to eight weeks? Why?"

"It's very important that Mr Crumbs has new shoes, and his feet trimmed regularly," Mrs Cox explained. "Otherwise he could get sore feet, or even damage them."

"Oh, I see," said Emily.

"Then there's vet's bills," Mrs Cox continued. "Including worming, vaccinations and having his teeth checked regularly. It's difficult to put a figure on that, it depends what needs treating at the time."

Ben tapped away on his calculator. "Food, bedding and shoes comes to approximately eight hundred and thirty-five pounds a year. That's about sixteen pounds a week. Plus we need to put something aside for vet's bills."

"We're only going to have twelve pounds," said Emily. "It's not enough."

Laura sighed but she wasn't going to be put off. "We can do two jobs a week each," she said quickly. "That'll bring in another eight pounds."

"Two jobs is the maximum," said Sanjay.

"We've got to leave time to see to Mr Crumbs and do our homework. And don't forget I have to help my dad, too."

"Two jobs each brings it up to twenty pounds a week," said Ben. "We'd be okay for his keep – and probably the vet's bills. But there's still his accommodation. We don't know how much that's going to cost."

"I'll make some enquiries for you," said Mrs Cox. "I'm sure we can find somewhere nearby to keep him."

"I do hope so," said Laura, gently washing Mr Crumbs's nose and muzzle with a sponge.

Then Ben untied him, led him into the stable and took his head collar off,

Tiggy immediately jumped up on to the stable door. Mr Crumbs came over to greet the tabby cat and she rubbed herself against his nose before jumping down and settling in the straw.

"Mrs Worth at the post office has offered to take Tiggy in," said Mrs Cox. "But Tiggy and Crumbs are really going to miss each other."

Laura wondered if they could find a way to keep them together, but she didn't say anything – not yet.

Mrs Cox picked up the empty mugs. "If there's anything I can do to help, let me know," she said, and headed indoors.

Laura and Ben picked up a shovel and a bucket.

"Right," said Ben. "Now for the fun job! We've got to pick up his droppings from the field. We have to keep it clean."

"Manure!" cried Emily.

"Er – yes, Emily," said Sanjay. "That *is* what it's called."

"No, silly. What I mean is – my Uncle Jack buys manure from the garden centre to put on his allotment," said Emily. "And so do lots of other people. We could sell the manure to raise money."

"Brilliant," said Laura, laughing. "What do you think you can manage, Mr Crumbs? A bucketful a day?"

Mr Crumbs tossed his head and walked over to his hay net.

"You've embarrassed him now," said Sanjay.

Ben was making notes. "We could probably get between twenty-five and fifty pence a bucket for it," he said. "I bet we could earn one or even two pounds a week. Well done, Emily, that's a great idea."

Emily beamed at him.

"We need to think up more ideas like that," said Sanjay, as they headed for the field. "Our biggest problem is going to be raising six months' money up front. We haven't got much time."

Laura thought about it as they went about their task. It would be difficult, as Mr Crumbs had to be re-homed shortly after Christmas. There were only four-and-a-half weeks to Christmas, and if they were lucky they might have one or two weeks afterwards.

"What we need is a big money-making idea," said Ben.

"How about putting on a Christmas show?" Emily suggested.

But the others weren't keen – they thought it would be too complicated.

Then Laura had a brainwave. "A Christmas Bazaar!" she cried. "We can make things – and collect stuff from other people to sell."

"That's a great idea," said Emily, as they hurried back to the stable. "I bet we'd make lots of money."

Mr Crumbs heard them come back and put his head over the stable door to join in the conversation.

"We'll need somewhere to hold it," said Sanjay, patting the pony's neck. "A hall or something."

"Halls cost money to hire," said Ben.

"It needs to be somewhere cheap," said Laura. "Somewhere cheap – and different."

"Something like a big shed, or a barn?" said Emily.

"A barn would be great," said Laura. "We could decorate it and make it really Christmassy."

Mr Crumbs tossed his head and gave a little whinny. He obviously agreed.

"That old man next door to you's got a barn," said Sanjay. "D'you think he'd let us use it?"

"I dunno," said Laura. "But it's worth a try." Mr Jakes had lived next door to them for about six months, but they hardly ever saw him. His house was a converted farm cottage and in his back garden was a big, old barn that had been on the land when he bought it from the farmer. He sometimes said hello to Mum or Dad but he always seemed very unfriendly towards the children, and avoided them whenever possible.

"I can't imagine he uses the barn for anything," said Laura. "And surely for a good cause like this. . ."

"We'll go and ask him tomorrow morning," said Ben. "After we've seen to Mr Crumbs."

Chapter 4

Mr Jakes

"I'm not usually up this early on a Sunday morning," said Emily, yawning, as they put the stable-cleaning equipment away.

Laura smiled. "You'll get used to it." They started down the drive and paused by the gate to the field. Mr Crumbs was concentrating hard in his efforts to pull the hay out of the hay net they'd hung up for him. He swung his head round to them, chewing thoughtfully.

Laura scratched him under his forelock. "Your stable's all done, so we're off now. See you this evening, Crumbs."

Sanjay stroked him. "Doesn't he get cold out here?"

"No, his coat is nice and thick, and it hasn't been clipped," said Ben. "But if it gets really cold we put a rug on him."

"Oh, right," said Sanjay, as they left. "Well, Emily, we've had our first lesson in mucking out."

"Yeah, we're learning fast," said Emily. "I'm so glad my mum okayed it for me to own him with you three. Even if she did agree with Ben and Laura's dad that we had to get at least six months' money up front."

"My mum and dad were actually quite keen," said Sanjay. "They said the responsibility would do me good."

"I'm really glad they agreed too," said Ben. "If this is going to be possible, it'll need the four of us."

"Of course it's going to be possible," said Laura. "Now come on, let's go and ask Mr Jakes about his barn."

There was no answer when they knocked on Mr Jakes' front door.

They tried round the back but there was no sign of him there either.

"He's probably gone out," said Sanjay.

"Let's have a quick peek inside the barn," suggested Emily. "We might be able to see what it looks like."

They had just reached the barn when the door opened and Mr Jakes came hurrying out. "What are you kids up to?" he shouted.

Ben, Emily and Sanjay all jumped back, but Laura stood her ground. "Good morning, Mr Jakes," she said. "We were –

er – just wondering if we could use your barn for our Christmas Bazaar."

"I don't want kids round here, causing trouble," said Mr Jakes, hastily pulling the barn door closed behind him. "Clear off."

"But—"

"There's nothing here to interest you. Don't come near my barn again."

"What an unfriendly man," said Emily, as they hurried away.

"Why's he so touchy about an old barn?" asked Sanjay.

"Maybe he's a bank robber," said Emily. "And he's got all his loot stashed away in there. He looks like a crook – he's got shifty eyes."

"Well, we've got more important things to worry about than him," said Laura.

"Such as where else to hold our bazaar – and where we can keep Mr Crumbs," said Sanjay. "Obviously no point in asking Mr Jakes if he can live in his barn."

"Wouldn't be any good anyway," said Ben. "Mr Crumbs needs at least an acre of field to be turned out into during the day."

"There must be loads of other places," said Laura. "Like – like the farm next door. They must have got another barn if they sold this one to Mr Jakes."

"Okay, we'll go and ask," said Ben.

They trudged next door, trying to remain cheerful. But the farmer didn't have a barn they could use for the bazaar. And neither did he have any land he could rent out for Mr Crumbs to live on. Even Emily's offer of free manure towards the rent couldn't sway him.

They headed off home for lunch. It wasn't a very good start to the day, but they all had fundraising plans for the afternoon. Sanjay had arranged for him and Ben to wash his dad's car for two pounds. Emily was going to walk a neighbour's dog. And Laura had offered to do some housework for an elderly friend of her mum's.

They agreed to meet afterwards to get Mr Crumbs in for the night and to discuss how they'd got on.

Laura was the first to arrive. Mr Crumbs immediately left his pow-wow with the goats and trotted over to her. She slipped the lead-rope round his neck and gave him a piece of apple.

"Good boy," she said, as she slid the headcollar over his nose. She lifted the strap behind his ears and buckled it up. "You're such a good boy."

Laura walked alongside his head and led him over to the stable. "We haven't found anywhere to keep you yet – but we've got loads more ideas," she told him.

Tiggy greeted them outside the stable and Laura fetched the grooming kit. She took out the hoof pick and ran her hand down Mr Crumbs's front leg to his fetlock. He obediently lifted his foot so she could pick out his hoof. "I wonder where the others have got to?" she said. "I'm dreading telling them how much I earned this afternoon."

Laura had finished grooming Mr Crumbs and was giving him his drink of water by the time Ben and Sanjay arrived. They held out four pound coins. "We washed two cars," said Sanjay. "One of my neighbours saw us washing Dad's car and asked us to do hers as well."

"How much did you get, Laura?" Ben asked.

It was time to own up. "Ten pence."

"Ten pence?"

Laura explained how she'd cleaned the whole of the lady's kitchen, including the cooker. Then the old lady had thanked her and given her ten pence. "I don't know if she didn't hear me properly or if she hadn't got any money," said Laura. "But I didn't like to ask for more."

Ben laughed. "Let's hope Emily did better." He went off with Sanjay to get Mr Crumbs's food.

But Emily arrived with no money. The dog she was walking had run off and she'd had to get the owner to help find it. So of course, he hadn't paid her.

Ben did a quick calculation while Mr Crumbs noisily searched out the carrots in his bucket of food. With the one pound contribution each from their pocket money, they had raised eight pounds and ten pence. "We've got a long way to go," he said.

Laura sighed. "Let's go home and start working out what we can make for our bazaar."

"Okay," said Ben. "We'll have a meeting of the Mr Crumbs Committee on Wednesday evening and see what we've all come up with."

Mr Crumbs finished his food and Laura

washed his nose and orange lips with the sponge. "Don't worry, this is only the first weekend," she whispered to him, as she led him into his stable. "There's still loads of time."

He gave a little whinny and she was sure he understood her.

Chapter 5

We Can't Give up

They had a half-day off school on Wednesday so Laura took the opportunity of an extra ride on Mr Crumbs. During the winter she usually only got to ride him at weekends, because it got dark so early.

Emily was doing some shopping for an elderly neighbour and Ben and Sanjay had gone to have a chat with Mrs Cox.

Laura liked her time alone with Mr Crumbs. She gave him a gentle squeeze with her legs. "Walk on, Mr Crumbs."

He obediently set off round the field.

Somehow the field, and the surrounding area, looked different from between Mr Crumbs's ears. It was as though she was seeing it from his view.

She gave him another squeeze. "Trot on, Mr Crumbs."

They trotted round for a while and then slowed to a walk. Mrs Cox was happy for Laura to exercise Mr Crumbs on her own. She knew she could trust her just to stay in the field. Laura's riding hat had been a birthday present, and Mrs Cox had given her and Ben riding boots that had belonged to her children.

Laura brought Mr Crumbs to a halt. She leaned forward to pat his neck.

"That was great. Good boy." She slipped her feet out of the stirrups and dismounted.

"We're having a meeting of the Mr Crumbs Committee tonight," she told him, as she ran the stirrups up the stirrup leathers. Then she slackened the girth. "Ben wants to talk about his business plan and we're going to discuss our ideas for the bazaar."

She led him off towards the stable. "But we haven't found anywhere to hold the bazaar yet. The village hall is much too expensive – and in any case it's booked. And so are both the church halls."

Laura tied Mr Crumbs up and took his saddle off. "But the rest of the fundraising's going quite well. Ben washed one of Dad's client's cars yesterday and I cleaned the inside. We got two pounds each. Sanjay earned two pounds for cleaning his dad's shop window and Emily should get two pounds today."

Mr Crumbs tilted his head, peering out of the corner of his eye to see if any food was coming yet.

Laura loved it when he did that. She laughed and gave him a carrot. "We've already found a customer for your manure," she said, as his soft lips searched her hand to make sure he didn't miss any bits. "Emily's uncle. And he knows lots of other people with allotments."

Sanjay arrived and said that Ben had gone straight home to work on his business plan. He helped Laura groom and feed Mr Crumbs and clean the riding tack. Then they headed home, both looking forward to the meeting that evening.

Ben spread his papers in front of him on the table. He took his glasses off and polished them on his jumper. "I don't think we can do it."

"What?" Laura looked at him in horror.

"It's just not practical," said Ben, replacing his glasses. "Mrs Cox has been asking around and she says the very cheapest accommodation we're likely to find – just a field and basic shelter – is ten pounds a week."

"Not that she's found any that's available," said Sanjay. "And neither have we."

"Therefore, with ten pounds a week for food and bedding, six pounds towards shoeing, two pounds – at least – towards vet's bills and ten pounds for accommodation, if we can find any, that makes twenty-eight pounds a week," said Ben. "We can't earn twenty-eight pounds a week."

"But that's twenty-eight pounds between four of us," said Laura. "Seven pounds each."

"I can give an extra one pound a week," said Emily. "Mum got a pay rise and she said if I keep my bedroom clean and tidy she'll give me another one pound a week pocket money."

"And I don't mind making my contribution three pounds," said Sanjay. "As I get more than the rest of you."

"Well, I'm perfectly happy to give two pounds a week from my pocket money," said Laura. "There's nothing I want to spend my money on more than Mr Crumbs."

Ben wrote it all down and reluctantly agreed to raise his to one pound fifty. "That makes eight pounds fifty a week," he said.

"And the manure," said Emily.

"Okay, let's say an average of one pound fifty a week for the manure," said Ben. "So that's ten pounds a week plus what we earn."

"And at two jobs a week each that's another sixteen pounds," said Laura. "So that's twenty'six pounds a week – we're almost there. We could make the bazaar an annual event to raise the rest of the money."

Ben did some more calculations. "We'll need to make at least a hundred and four pounds profit from the bazaar every year. But don't forget we've got to raise the first six months' money in just a few weeks. That's around seven hundred pounds. I just don't see how we can do that."

"Oh, for goodness' sake, let's at least try!" said Laura. She ran up to her room and came back with her piggy bank. "I was saving for a new bike but I want Mr Crumbs more." The coins clattered all over the table as she shook it.

Ben counted it out. "Twenty'seven pounds and sixteen pence."

"I'll ask for money for Christmas instead of a present," said Laura. "And for my next birthday. And I don't care how hard I have to work. I don't want anything except Mr Crumbs. We can't give up."

"I don't want to give up," said Emily.

"No, let's give it a bit longer," said Sanjay.

"All right," said Ben. "We'll keep trying for a while. I suggest we open a savings account at the bank to keep the money in. At least it will be earning some interest."

"Good idea," said Laura. "Now what about the bazaar? I've got my list of ideas here." She took out a piece of paper. "I thought we could cut out gift tags from old Christmas cards, and make tree decorations – I've seen some ideas in a magazine. Make fluffy spiders and chicks out of old wool, and have a Guess the Number of Sweets in the Jar competition."

"Great," said Emily. "Me next. I thought of making fudge and coconut ice –Mum's got some really easy recipes. Making peg bags, and having a lucky dip –we can buy some little gifts cheap from the market and wrap them up. And we could sell refreshments."

"I thought of painting some ordinary

cheap pots to plant bulbs in," said Sanjay. "And I could make paperweights, plaster models and table decorations."

"And perhaps you could design some posters to advertise the bazaar, Sanjay," said Ben. "As you're the one that's best at artistic-type things." Then he got out his own list. "Christmas cards," he read. "Buying up large boxes from the market and putting them into nice smaller packages. And doing the same with wrapping paper. And we could sell second-hand books, videos and CDs that we can collect from friends and neighbours."

"Brilliant," said Laura. "And perhaps Mr Crumbs could give pony rides."

"Good idea. We could charge fifty pence a ride," said Ben. "I'll make a note of all the ideas and how much we could charge."

"There's only four weeks to Christmas," said Sanjay. "So we'd better get a move on."

"Yes. This has got to be the biggest and best bazaar ever," said Laura. "It's got to make loads and loads of money."

Chapter 6

More Ideas

On Saturday morning Laura and Emily met up to see to Mr Crumbs while Ben and Sanjay delivered manure to the allotments. Mrs Cox usually saw to her pony on weekday mornings and the children came every evening after school and twice at weekends. Soon – when Mr Crumbs belonged to them – they would have to get up early to see to him before school as well. Laura couldn't wait.

Mr Crumbs pawed the ground, impatient for his feed. His warm breath rose like steam in the morning air.

Emily finished brushing his tail and wiped under his dock with a sponge. "It was a shame about Marsham Hall, wasn't it?" she said.

"Yes, I'd really got my hopes up about that," said Laura, as she gave Mr Crumbs his food bucket. Marsham Hall was a big house just outside town and the owner kept three horses of her own. "Such a pity she didn't have room for Mr Crumbs as well."

They'd also tried Church Farm, Westdene Farm and Mr Brown who ran a market garden – but they hadn't had any luck there either.

Emily giggled as she watched Mr Crumbs searching out the carrots in his bucket. "I love the way he does that," she said. "He's a real carrot-oholic."

Laura smiled and patted the pony's warm

neck. "I hope Ben and Sanjay have some luck at the vet's when they've finished delivering the manure. A vet must have somewhere to keep large animals that have to stay in."

"Yes, and if not, they're bound to know of somewhere else we can keep him," said Emily. "They must know all the farmers round here."

Laura led Mr Crumbs out to his field and saw to his hay net and water while Emily made a start on mucking out the stable. On Saturday mornings they removed all the straw and disinfected the floor.

As soon as they'd finished, the two girls made their way to *Fowler's Family Restaurant*. Sanjay's mum had suggested they might have a room they could use for their bazaar.

"I'm really sorry but I'm using the room for extra seating now," said Mr Fowler. "But I think it's great what you kids are trying to do. When you do find somewhere, I'll give you a voucher for a meal for two as a raffle prize."

"Wow, thanks," said Emily.

"Why don't you try the *Rose and Crown Inn?*" he suggested. "They've definitely got a functions room they let out."

But the landlord of the *Rose and Crown Inn* couldn't help them either. "We have got a room," he said. "But I'm afraid it's fully booked for Christmas parties until the end of January."

It was disappointing, but encouraged by the offer from the restaurant, Laura plucked up the courage to ask if he would consider donating a raffle prize.

"I'll give you two bottles of wine," said the landlord. "You'll have to get your parents to collect them though."

"A raffle's a great idea," said Laura, as they left. "You make lots of money with a raffle."

On the way home they called in at the hardware store (who said they couldn't give them anything) and then the greengrocer's, who promised them a basket of fruit.

As they arrived at Laura's house, Emily spotted Mr Jakes carrying two large boxes of "loot" into his barn. "Did you see the shifty way he looked around him? I bet he is a bank robber. Hey!" Emily grabbed Laura's arm. "D'you think there might be a reward for his capture?"

"A what?"

"A reward." Emily's eyes were shining. "Just think, it would solve all our money worries for Mr Crumbs."

"Oh, Emily, Mr Jakes couldn't possibly be a—" Laura started, but Emily wasn't listening.

"We ought to spy on him – see if we can get any evidence." Emily crept over to the hedge to peer through. She turned back suddenly, her eyes wide. "Hey! I just heard someone crying out. It came from the barn."

"Honestly, Emily, your imagination gets worse all the time," Laura giggled. "It was just a chicken. There are loads on the farm. Now come on."

She ushered her indoors and they found Ben and Sanjay in the kitchen looking through the adverts in the local paper. They hadn't had any luck at the vet's but the vet said they could advertise for somewhere to keep Mr Crumbs on his notice board.

"We thought about putting an advert in the paper as well," said Ben.

"And in my dad's chemist's shop window," said Sanjay. "And the post office."

"Great," said Laura. "Let's write some out after lunch."

"We've got to make ourselves a sandwich," said Ben. "Mum's doing a fitting for two bridesmaids in the living room."

"They must be the ones in red velvet," said Laura. "Mum was working on their dresses yesterday."

They heard the steady chug of Dad's vintage Daimler as it pulled up in the drive. He'd been to do a wedding over in Stanton, about twenty miles away.

Dad opened the kitchen door. "You kids couldn't do me a favour, could you? Wash and polish the Daimler? I've just driven down a really muddy lane and the car's got filthy."

"How much?" asked Laura. This was business, after all.

"A fiver, if you can do it right away," said Dad. "I need the car for another wedding at three o'clock, and I've got to fix Dr Johnson's BMW."

"Oh well, lunch will have to wait," said Ben, as they filled buckets with hot water and fetched old cloths. They started work on the muddy paintwork and Laura and Emily told the two boys about the raffle prizes.

"That's great," said Ben. "I've been doing some figures on the bazaar. The packets of gift tags we've made should sell for fifty pence each." He wiped the water splashes off his glasses with his sleeve. "So that's eighteen pounds if we sell all thirty-six packets. And the fluffy spiders and chicks could bring in twenty-five pounds – if we can make fifty."

Emily giggled. "Only if we can make the chicks look less like vultures."

"Tonight we ought to wrap up all those notebooks, pencils and plastic toys we got from the market for the lucky dip," said Sanjay.

"And we should make a start on the big boxes of Christmas cards," said Laura. "I thought we could put twelve in a packet and maybe stick tiny crêpe-paper bows on the front to make them look nice."

The car was soon washed and dried.

The boys polished the paintwork while Laura and Emily started on the big chrome headlights.

Then they swept the confetti out of the interior and put fresh white ribbons on the front. It looked good when they'd finished. Even Dad was pleased – and he was very fussy.

"You've done a really good job," he said, handing a five-pound note to Ben.

Laura watched him reverse the car into the garage and had an idea. Dad's garage was big – not really as big as they wanted, but they could make do. "Dad, as you're out most Saturdays at weddings, could we use the garage for our bazaar?"

"No, Laura. Even if I have two weddings, like today, the car is back here at some point, and I need to keep it under cover," said Dad. "And there's usually a customer's car in the garage too."

"Shame, the garage would have been good," said Sanjay, as they went indoors. "But at least it's lunch time now – at last."

As they ate, they wrote out the advertisements for the vet's, the local newspaper, Sanjay's shop and the post office.

"What about the library?" said Sanjay. "They've got a noticeboard."

"Yes. And they might have a room for the bazaar," said Laura.

"Let's go there first then," said Ben. "There's only three-and-a-half weeks to Christmas now."

Chapter 7

A Breakthrough

Laura paused from sifting out the soiled straw with the fork to watch Mr Crumbs. Emily was sitting on him and Ben was leading her round the field.

He's so beautiful, she thought. *We've got to raise the money to keep him.*

They hadn't had any luck with a room for the bazaar at the library yesterday. But they had put up one of their notices asking for a field and stable.

Mrs Cox had got a date for moving out now – the eighth of January. So they had to find somewhere for Mr Crumbs to live before then.

Laura sighed and went back to forking up the straw. "Hey, mind out, Tiggy," she said, as she spotted the tabby cat curled up in the corner. "You don't want to be put on the muck heap, do you?"

Tiggy reluctantly got up, stretched herself and strolled outside.

Laura wheeled the full wheelbarrow round the back and had just put the fresh straw in the stable when Ben brought Emily back on Mr Crumbs. Laura held the pony's reins and stroked his nose while Ben helped Emily to dismount.

There was such trust in his velvet-brown eyes as he looked at her. "I won't let you down," she told him.

Laura took her hard hat from Emily and swung herself into the saddle.

She walked Mr Crumbs back to the field and leaned over and patted his strong neck. "There's still time to raise the money," she whispered to him. "And to find somewhere to keep you."

She gave him a gentle squeeze with her legs. "Trot on, Mr Crumbs."

They had a busy week. Every evening, after they'd seen to Mr Crumbs and had dinner, the four friends met up to work on things for their bazaar. But they still couldn't find anywhere to hold it.

Laura was glad when it was Friday – she was looking forward to spending time over the weekend with Mr Crumbs. She and Emily waited for Ben and Sanjay after school as they usually did, so they could all go together to see to Mr Crumbs.

But the boys were late coming out and Laura was getting impatient. "Where have they got to?" she asked Emily. "We've got to see to Mr Crumbs, and sew the legs on all those fluffy spiders for the bazaar later."

"They didn't say they weren't coming with us," said Emily.

Laura sighed and went back into school to look for them. She was tired – they were all tired.

She spotted Ben in the hall. His class was performing a nativity play for the rest of the school and they were obviously rehearsing.

Ben saw her and came to the door. "We'll be about another half an hour," he said. "You'd better go on without us."

"Why didn't you tell me you had a rehearsal?" Laura demanded. "Emily and I could almost have finished Mr Crumbs by now. And we've got loads more work to do this evening. There's only two-and-a-half weeks to Christmas now." She felt so tired and her head was beginning to ache.

"Sorry," said Ben. "I forgot."

"You forgot?" Laura snapped. "The trouble with you is that you don't really care, do you? Oh, you come along and do a few bits and pieces. And you write figures in your notebook. But you're not committed, are you?"

Laura didn't wait for an answer – she stormed out of the school to where Emily was waiting for her.

Emily did her best to cheer her friend up as they walked along to Mrs Cox's and Laura had calmed down a bit by the time they got there. But Mr Crumbs always sensed when Laura wasn't happy. Emily was fixing the hay net in the stable and Laura went to untie the lead rope to take him inside.

Suddenly Mr Crumbs brought his head down and rested it on her shoulder. She reached up and stroked the side of his face. His warmth and familiar smell were comforting.

The two girls paused outside Laura's house and Laura even managed a smile when Emily spotted a ginger cat going into Mr Jakes's garden.

"I wouldn't go in there if I were you," Emily told it. "He'll probably eat you – or make you into fur gloves."

"Emily, that's awful," she giggled.

Emily left to go home for dinner and Laura went indoors and straight up to her room. It was full of things they'd made for the bazaar, as well as second-hand books and CDs they'd collected from friends and neighbours, and a Christmas cake Emily's mum had made them. Ben had decided they'd make more money from the cake if they asked people to guess the weight rather than just sell it.

They'd got a jar of sweets from the newsagents for people to guess how many there were. And *The Bookstore* had given them a book token for the raffle.

Laura slumped down on the bed and looked at the stacks of boxes. What was the use of it all if they hadn't got anywhere to hold the bazaar? For the first time, she felt really discouraged.

The door opened and Ben came in. Laura ignored him – she was still feeling cross.

"How about the school hall to hold the bazaar in?" he said. "And for free?"

"What? I mean – how?" Laura wasn't sure she'd heard right. "You're not joking, are you?"

"No." Ben adjusted his glasses. "I thought about things after you'd gone. And how hard you'd worked – it's all down to you, really."

"Look, I'm sorry – about what I said," said Laura. "We've all worked really hard. I was tired and – oh, just tell me what happened."

"Well, I knew the school hall is only usually used for school events," said Ben. "But I thought it was worth a try, and I told Miss Featherstone all about Mr Crumbs."

"And she said we could use the hall? Just like that?" said Laura.

"Not quite 'just like that'," said Ben. "She was impressed with what we've been doing – and she just happens to love horses. So she went off and made a couple of phone calls and then came back to say it was all okay – for Saturday week. The fifteenth of December."

Chapter 8

Busy Days

The next day, Saturday, was really busy. All four of them spent the whole day working on things for the bazaar. But none of them felt tired any more.

When they went to bring Mr Crumbs in for the night, Laura and Ben left Emily and Sanjay to groom and feed him on their own while they cleaned up his field.

Both Emily and Sanjay were quite competent now and the pony was happily sorting out the carrots in his food bucket when Laura and Ben returned.

"We've definitely reached a turning point now," said Sanjay.

Laura nodded and patted Mr Crumbs. "Bet you anything someone will ring this weekend and offer us a field and a stable."

"Yeah – for practically nothing as well," Emily chuckled.

Mr Crumbs finally lifted his nose out of the bucket and Sanjay gently washed it with the sponge.

The pony had picked up on their excitement and looked from one to the other. Then he tossed his head and whinnied.

Ben laughed and patted him. "It's great, your mums offering to do the refreshments at the bazaar," he said to Emily and Sanjay.

"Yeah, they got together this morning

about it," said Sanjay. "My mum's making lots of different savouries and Emily's mum is making cakes."

"And they're going to serve tea and coffee, and orange juice," said Emily.

"That's great," said Laura, but she felt a bit awkward. Emily's and Sanjay's mums were helping and Sanjay's dad was donating a box of bath toiletries for the raffle. But her mum and dad hadn't offered anything.

Dad had been out doing a wedding today and she'd hardly seen Mum. The two bridesmaids with the red velvet dresses – and the bride – had been round in the morning for a final fitting and since then Mum had been shut away in her workroom. They were both obviously too busy to help.

Emily started to lead Mr Crumbs into the stable, but halfway there he resisted and turned to look at Laura.

Laura patted him. "Go on, Crumbs. Emily knows what she's doing."

Mr Crumbs obediently went inside and Emily took off his headcollar. She closed the half-door on the stable behind her and he hung his head over it so that he could be included. He hated to miss anything.

Mrs Cox arrived with their hot chocolate. "I'm so excited about your bazaar. It's really looking hopeful that you might be able to keep Mr Crumbs now," she told them. "Oh, I know the sanctuary would take good care of him but I'd much rather he stayed with you."

Laura smiled at her. "Thanks."

"I only wish I could help you out

financially, but all my money's tied up in the move to Australia," said Mrs Cox. "But if you'd like any of the tack – saddles, bridles, that sort of thing – you're welcome to it. And all the stable-cleaning equipment."

"Wow, thanks," said Laura. "That'll be a terrific help."

The next week was spent in a frenzy of activity. They worked like crazy to finish off the things they were making. Mrs Cox was clearing out her house ready to move and she gave them more books and lots of bric-a-brac to sell. Emily's uncle promised them produce from his allotment and some plants from his greenhouse.

There was no doubt about Ben's commitment now. He spent hours making Christmas decorations to sell. He made bells, angels, Christmas trees and robins, which he cut out of card. Then he painted them, covered them in glitter and added thread to hang them up.

Laura and Emily bought dozens of hyacinth, crocus and daffodil bulbs from the market and planted them in Sanjay's brightly painted pots.

Sanjay painted banners and posters to advertise the bazaar. They put them up everywhere anyone would allow them to, including three in the school. He also painted some large stones with brightly-coloured patterns, to be used as paperweights.

They all made table decorations out of logs and holly and Emily made fudge and coconut ice. Laura and Ben wrapped up another fifty lucky dips. They decorated a large box with crêpe paper, and filled it with shredded newspaper to hide the gifts.

On Friday evening everything was packed up and Sanjay's dad brought his car round to take it all to the hall. "Looks like this lot will take two trips," he said.

Then Emily's mum arrived to take Emily to pick up the raffle prizes they'd been promised.

Laura and Ben's dad was still in the garage and their mum was in her workroom – she'd hardly come out all week.

Laura and Ben called out to them as they left. "We're off to the school now." But they didn't come out to say goodbye.

Miss Featherstone was waiting for them at the hall. She seemed quite excited as she helped them carry in the boxes. "I can't believe how much stuff you've got," she said.

The caretaker had already put out tables for them, and Laura immediately started arranging the Christmas cards and gift tags on one of them.

They'd just finished unloading Sanjay's dad's car when, to everyone's surprise, Laura and Ben's mum and dad turned up too. Dad's car was piled up with the rest of their goods.

Mum and Dad unloaded everything from the car and helped arrange it on the tables. Just as they finished unpacking the last of the goods, Mum handed Laura a large box.

Laura opened it to see six dolls all dressed as brides. Mum had used the leftover material from all the wedding dresses she'd made. Under a layer of tissue were eight soft Father Christmases, made from the leftover red velvet from the bridesmaids' dresses. So that's what she'd been doing all week.

"Oh, Mum." Laura flung her arms round her mother. "Thanks."

"And this," said Mum, handing her an envelope. "It's a voucher for your raffle. I talked Dad into giving a free ride in his Daimler."

Laura was overjoyed. Everything was going so well. Then an awful thought struck her. "S'posing," she said, "just supposing – no one comes."

Chapter 9

The Mr Crumbs
Christmas Bazaar

They were up extra early on Saturday morning. Ben, Emily and Sanjay went straight to the school hall to put the finishing touches to the stalls and help set out the refreshments.

Laura went to see to Mr Crumbs and help Mrs Cox get him ready for the pony rides he was going to give at the bazaar.

He immediately sensed the excitement and they had trouble getting him to stand still while Laura painted hoof oil on his hooves to make them shiny.

Then he tried to eat the tinsel they were attaching to the browband at the top of his bridle.

"He probably thinks he's going to a gymkhana," Mrs Cox chuckled, as they entwined red and green ribbons into his mane and tail. "We used to enter him with the children when they were young."

Laura changed her clothes and packed some hay and his water bucket in a bag, along with plenty of carrots for treats during the day.

Then she mounted up and leaned forward to give Mr Crumbs a hug. "You're so smart. You're a real Christmas pony today."

Mrs Cox led him along the road as Laura had only ever ridden him in the field. Laura looked around her and, once again, was

amazed at how different – how beautiful –
the world looked from up on his back.

When they reached the school she was
relieved to see lots of people waiting to go
in. And a queue had already formed at the
notice they'd put up for the pony rides.

"Isn't he beautiful," said one little girl,
as they approached.

"I've got one pound," said a boy. "So I
can have two rides."

Mrs Cox smiled. "I can see I'm going to
be very busy today."

Laura dismounted and fetched Mr
Crumbs some water. Then she gave him
a special hug. "I love you, Mr Crumbs. Be
a good boy today."

Hanging over the entrance to the hall
was Sanjay's masterpiece. A huge banner
which read:

The Mr Crumbs
CHRISTMAS BAZAAR
10'o clock today

Inside, the hall looked incredible with all the decorations up and the tables piled high with goods. Even though she'd seen it almost finished the night before it still took Laura's breath away.

"Is everyone ready?" she asked.

Everyone nodded or called out "yes" from behind their tables.

"Right, I'll open the doors." She took a deep breath. "This bazaar is now open," she declared.

The day passed in a haze of activity. All the children in the school must have come – and brought their parents.

All the bride dolls and the Father Christmases were sold very quickly. Laura noticed that several adults who bought them quickly hid them under their coats or in their bags – they were obviously Christmas presents.

Every time she looked up she could see Mr Crumbs going past the window with yet another child on his back, He really looked as though he was enjoying the company and all the attention.

Rebecca, who was in Laura's class, won the sweets by guessing how many were in the jar. And the butcher's wife guessed the correct weight of the Christmas cake.

The raffle was an incredible success and made a hundred and two pounds. Mr Crumbs himself made twenty-five pounds. He could have made much more but Mrs

Cox kept the number of rides down to fifty and made sure he had regular breaks.

There wasn't much left by the time they finally closed the doors. And all that remained on the refreshment table were empty plates and a couple of tea bags.

Ben went to help Mrs Cox take Mr Crumbs home and settle him for the night while the rest of them cleared up.

"Well done," said Miss Featherstone. "That was a big success. Do you think you've raised enough money?"

"We haven't counted it all yet," said Laura. "But thank you so much for helping and for arranging for us to use the hall."

"That's all right – I admire you for what you're doing," said Miss Featherstone. "As I love horses myself, I can understand why you want to keep Mr Crumbs – he's a beautiful pony."

"I don't suppose there's anywhere to keep him here?" said Laura. "A field at the back of the school maybe? Everyone at school loved him today."

"I'd love to help but I'm afraid it's impossible. We can't keep Mr Crumbs on school property," said the teacher. "But I've been around horses for most of my life, so when you do find somewhere, if you need a hand with anything, I'd be pleased to help."

"Thanks," said Laura. "That's great." Now they had someone to go to for advice. And maybe Miss Featherstone could teach Emily and Sanjay to ride, and even help Laura and Ben improve their skills.

It was quite late by the time they got

home but Ben wouldn't go to bed until they had counted all the money. They'd made an incredible five hundred and seventy-eight pounds and fifty pence profit. Added to what they'd already saved they now had six hundred and eighty-three pounds and seventy-six pence. Almost enough for six months' keep.

Laura tumbled into bed, exhausted. But she knew she wouldn't sleep, her mind was too active. They were almost there – if only they could find somewhere to keep Mr Crumbs. If only someone would read one of their adverts and ring about a field and shelter for him.

They were bound to . . . it would happen next week . . . their luck was turning after all.

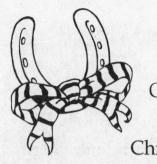

Chapter 10

Christmas Eve

School broke up for Christmas on Wednesday and the four friends concentrated their efforts on finding somewhere to keep Mr Crumbs. The success of the bazaar had renewed their enthusiasm. They looked everywhere – asked everyone they could think of. They inquired at the council offices, the railway station, the water board – any place they thought could possibly have any land.

But there was nothing. And nobody phoned about their adverts.

"We're surrounded by fields," said Laura.

"I can't believe there's not one we can use for Mr Crumbs. Not even one he can share."

So they started looking further away. The one place they found was the riding stables over at Westhorpe. But they only did full board at a hundred pounds a week. Even Laura agreed that was impossible.

By Christmas Eve they were feeling very low. They'd never dreamed it would be so hard to find Mr Crumbs a new home. And Mrs Cox was leaving for Australia in two weeks. Time was running out.

At lunchtime it started snowing and everyone felt even more depressed – except for Emily. "We'll be able to earn more money now, snow-clearing," she explained.

The snow shower didn't last long but

it was heavy and covered everything in a soft white blanket.

They decided to go and see to Mr Crumbs a bit earlier that afternoon, to groom him and put his blanket on before it snowed again.

They trudged wearily up to his field. Mr Crumbs didn't hear them approach as he usually did because their footsteps were muffled by the snow. He was standing there looking really dejected.

"He's probably missing the goats," said Ben. "Maggie took them down to Sussex with her two days ago."

"Plus he senses that something's wrong," said Laura. It broke her heart to see him like this.

At the sound of their voices Mr Crumbs pricked up his ears. He tossed his head, whinnied loudly, and trotted over.

Sanjay put on his headcollar and gave him some cut-up apple. Then he led him over to the stable.

Laura started to pick out his hooves with the hoof pick while Sanjay went to see to his feed. Ben took Emily to fetch his stable rug as it had turned so cold.

"We've made our seven hundred pounds," Laura told Mr Crumbs. "Seven hundred and two pounds and thirty-four pence to be exact. Ben put Saturday's pocket money straight into the bank today."

She fetched the grooming brushes and started brushing the pony's golden coat with the dandy brush. He turned to look at her and she felt his warm, sweet breath on her face.

"All we need now is somewhere to keep you," said Laura, trying to sound cheerful.

"There's probably somewhere really obvious that we just haven't thought of yet."

She moved round in front of him. Mr Crumbs's dark velvet eyes were sad. "I can't fool you, can I?" she said. "You're too intelligent. You know things aren't looking too hopeful right now."

Mr Crumbs rested his head on Laura's shoulder.

Laura put her arms round his neck and they stood there for a while, enjoying each other's warmth and comfort.

"Don't worry, I won't let you go," said Laura.

"You might have to," Ben warned her, as he and Emily came back with the stable rug. "There just isn't anywhere to keep him."

Laura didn't answer. She knew she'd burst into tears if she did.

It was snowing quite heavily again by the time they left Mr Crumbs. They trudged homewards and paused outside Ben and Laura's house to say goodbye. "Looks like Mum and Dad are still out Christmas shopping," said Ben. "The car's not here—" He stopped as they heard a shout.

"It came from Mr Jakes's house," said Emily. "What's he up to?"

"Oh, I can't be bothered with him right now," said Ben.

"Just ignore him, Emily," said Laura wearily.

The shout came again.

"He's calling for help," said Sanjay.

They immediately ran round to see Mr Jakes lying in his drive.

"I slipped on the snow," he cried. "I think I've broken my leg."

They rushed to help him. His head was bleeding and his leg was twisted in a most peculiar position. "Can you sit up?" asked Emily, bending down to him.

He waved her away. "Don't bother with me. Get help for the dog."

They all looked at each other in surprise. They didn't know he had a dog.

"What dog?" Laura asked.

"In the barn," he said. "She's giving birth – but she's in difficulties. Get some help."

The four children raced round to the barn. The door was open and they cautiously peered inside.

As their eyes became accustomed to the darkness they could see a black dog lying on a bed of straw. And there was more. . .

"Look, in that cage over there," said Laura, as they ventured in. "It's an owl."

"With one eye," said Sanjay. "And look, over there. A rabbit – and a pigeon."

Something scurried to the side of a run in the corner. "A fox," breathed Ben. "And his leg is bandaged."

An elderly-looking ginger cat came to greet them and rubbed round their legs.

"It's the one you saw coming in here, Emily," said Laura.

Something was snoring in a box under a table and a chicken squawked from the other side of the barn. "And that's the chicken I heard," said Emily.

"What are they all doing here?" said

Sanjay, as the owl winked at him with its one eye.

"I don't know." Laura kneeled down beside the trembling dog. "But look at this poor dog. She really needs help."

Ben looked outside. "The back door of the house is open. I'll go and phone for some help."

Laura went back to see Mr Jakes. He was trying to drag himself up the drive on his bottom.

"You shouldn't move that leg," said Laura.

"Don't fuss about me," snapped the old man. "I told you to get help for the dog."

Ben appeared. "It's all under control. I've phoned for an ambulance for you," he told the old man. "And I've called a vet for the dog."

"What?" said Mr Jakes. "I'm not going to hospital. My animals need me – I can't just leave them. And I can't afford to have a vet come out. They charge a fortune for a call-out – and for an emergency. And this is both. Can't you get your parents to help or something?"

"Our parents are out," said Ben. "And we can't waste time trying to find someone who just might be able to help. That dog needs a vet," he added firmly. "And she needs one now."

"And we'll look after the animals if you have to stay in hospital," said Laura.

"You? You're just kids," said Mr Jakes. "I'm not letting you anywhere near my animals."

Sanjay put his hands on his hips indignantly. "We're not 'just kids'. And we know all about looking after ponies – so your smaller animals and a couple of birds shouldn't be a problem."

Ben took out his notebook and pencil. "We know about cats, dogs and chickens. Just tell us what to do with the others."

Mr Jakes winced in pain. "I suppose I haven't really got a choice – like this. I'll have to trust you." He quickly told them how to care for the owl, rabbit, fox and pigeon. The hedgehog – which was what the snoring from the box under the table was – was hibernating and wouldn't need any attention. "You will treat them kindly, won't you?" he added.

"Of course we will," said Emily.

"But I've got no money at all to pay the vet," said Mr Jakes. "I bet it will cost at least a hundred pounds – maybe more."

Laura looked down at him. His eyes were moist. And it wasn't from the pain – he really cared about his animals. He wasn't a horrible man like they'd thought at all. She shifted her feet. "We've got some money," she said quietly.

"But that's for Mr Crumbs," said Ben.

Chapter 11

Give the Kids a Chance

Mr Jakes was just being carried into the ambulance when the vet arrived. The decision to pay for him with some of their money hadn't taken long to make. They couldn't let the poor dog suffer and they knew it was important to move fast.

And as Emily said, they'd have a week and a half after Christmas to earn some more money. "We'll just have to work extra hard. "At least we can do some snow-clearing."

"It'll mean less time to look for somewhere for Mr Crumbs to live," said

Ben. "Especially now we've got to look after Mr Jakes's animals as well."

They waited silently at one side of the barn until the vet called them over. He explained that one of the puppies had died and was blocking the way for the others to be born. "It's a good job you called me when you did," he told them.

"Is the dog all right?" Laura asked him anxiously.

"She's fine now." He smiled at them. "And how's this for a Christmas present?" He pointed to two tiny puppies suckling from their mother.

"Oh, they're so sweet," said Emily.

"The black one's a boy and the sandy one's a girl," said the vet.

"We should think of names for them," said Ben.

Laura looked at the contented trio on the straw. There was something special, magical even, about a birth on Christmas Eve. "How about Mary and Joseph?" she suggested.

"Brilliant!" they all agreed.

Later, the hospital phoned to say Mr Jakes had to stay in. Dad was home and he offered to drive them there so they could tell him about the puppies.

They arrived just as Mr Jakes came back from having an X-ray. He didn't look anything like so fierce, lying in a hospital bed. His leg was badly broken and he had to have an operation that evening.

"Your dog's fine," Laura told him. "She's had two lovely puppies."

"We've called them Mary and Joseph,"

said Emily. "Oh – unless you'd rather call them something else."

"No, they're good names," said Mr Jakes. "But the money for the vet," he turned towards Laura's dad. "I can't repay you."

"I haven't paid anything," said Dad. "What have you kids been saying?"

"It's all right, Dad. We're paying," said Ben. "The vet's sending his bill after Christmas."

"You're paying?" said the old man. "How?"

Between them, the children explained about Mr Crumbs, including the reason they'd wanted to use his barn.

"Why didn't you say that was why you needed the barn?" he asked.

"You didn't exactly give us a chance," said Sanjay.

"No, you're right, I'm sorry. But I get very twitchy about anyone going near the barn, because of the animals," said Mr Jakes. "Some of them have already been badly treated. The dog was chucked out on to the streets by her owner – presumably because she was pregnant. And the fox was injured by boys throwing stones at it."

"We're not like that," said Ben indignantly.

"I know that now. And I'm so grateful to you for using your hard-earned money for my dog." Mr Jakes shifted uncomfortably in the bed. "But what about your pony? Where are you going to keep him?"

"We can't find anywhere," said Laura sadly.

"Well, providing you're going to look after him yourselves, he can live in my barn," said Mr Jakes. "I won't charge you anything."

"Wow!" said Laura, Emily and Sanjay together.

"It wouldn't be any good," said Ben quickly. "He's got to have at least an acre of field and you've got hardly any garden."

"The field out the back belongs to me," said Mr Jakes. "I bought it along with the farm cottage and the barn – it took all of my money. There was this donkey, you see – but she died before I could get her here. . ." His eyes misted over. "But it would be perfect for your pony."

Laura couldn't believe it. Mr Crumbs would be living just next-door! "Oh, that's brilliant! Thank you so much, Mr Jakes."

"Now steady on," said Dad. He'd gone quite pale. "You're going a bit fast here."

"But you promised!" Laura and Ben shouted at once.

"I didn't promise – I said I'd think about it," said Dad. "But I didn't really think—"

"You didn't think we could do it, did you?" said Laura. "But we have. We've got six months' money in advance and now we've got somewhere to keep him."

"Only we haven't got six months' money now," whispered Emily. "Not once we've paid the vet."

"Yes, we have," said Ben. "If we haven't got to pay any rent then we've got plenty of money." He whipped his calculator out.

"Without rent – for six months we only need about four hundred and sixty pounds to keep Mr Crumbs."

"And even if we have to pay the vet a

hundred pounds, we've still got six hundred and two pounds and thirty-four pence left," said Laura.

"Oh, come on, give the kids a chance," said Mr Jakes. "What they've achieved is incredible. What are you worried about?"

"Money – I can't afford to bail them out if they get into difficulties. I've only just started up my business. And I'm sure Emily's mum—"

Mr Jakes beckoned Dad closer and whispered something to him.

As Dad listened, a smile gradually spread across his face.

"What?" said Laura.

Chapter 12

The Christmas Pony

"Happy Christmas, Mr Crumbs." Laura took out the carrot-shaped Christmas present.

"That's a bit obvious, isn't it?" laughed Emily.

Mr Crumbs pawed the snow-covered ground impatiently as Laura unwrapped it for him. It was a perfect Christmas day. Snow on the ground, but bright and crisp. And best of all – they now had their very own pony.

"I couldn't be more pleased," said Mrs Cox. "Fancy Mr Jakes coming up trumps like that. I'd never have thought of asking him."

"He's actually quite friendly when you get talking to him," said Ben. "And he knows loads about animals."

"And he doesn't look so old when he's not scowling," said Sanjay. "He's only been retired for a few years."

Mr Jakes had told them how he'd been taking in lost, unwanted and injured animals since he'd moved there six months ago. He'd tried to keep it a secret because he didn't want people poking round and frightening the animals.

"Did you find out what Mr Jakes whispered to your dad to make him give in?" asked Sanjay.

"He pointed out that a pony and trap could be used for weddings," said Ben.

"Dad's already worked out that it would be much cheaper than a second vintage car – which was what he was aiming towards."

"Mr Crumbs used to love pulling our old trap," said Mrs Cox. She stroked the pony's nose. "You'd enjoy doing that again, wouldn't you, Crumbs? Lots of company, lots of exercise."

"I still can't believe it," said Emily. "Mr Jakes was the last person I thought would have helped us. I thought –" She gave a giggle. "I thought he was a bank robber."

They all laughed.

Ben fastened the pony's New Zealand rug on him to keep him warm and dry out in the snowy field.

"And we don't have to pay any rent, so we won't have to work so hard." Laura stroked Mr Crumbs's soft nose. "We'll be able to spend more time with you."

Mr Crumbs gave a soft whinny and tried to get in her pocket for the second hidden carrot.

Laura took it out and unwrapped it for him. They'd already decided to hold a Christmas bazaar every year and have a stall at the village summer fete. They still had to earn money, not only for Mr Crumbs's keep, but because they wanted to help with Mr Jakes's rescued animals too.

Laura gave Mr Crumbs another piece of carrot.

"He'll love it in the barn with all the other animals," said Sanjay. "Especially when our dads have built his stall at one end."

"And I can leave without worrying now," said Mrs Cox. "Knowing that Mr Crumbs will be happy and well cared for. But I'm going to miss you all."

"We'll write to you – often," said Laura. "And let you know how Mr Crumbs is getting on."

The pony crunched on his carrot with his ears pricked, listening to them.

He gave a little snicker as Tiggy appeared and rubbed herself against his back leg. Then he put his soft muzzle into Laura's hand to see if he'd missed any bits of carrot.

She kissed him on his nose. "And you know what else, Crumbs? Tiggy's coming too. Mr Jakes said it's okay."

Ben patted Mr Crumb's neck. "Mr Jakes is all right. He's just one of those people who gets on better with animals than with humans."

"But he wants us round there," said Laura. "And most important of all. . ." She reached up and whispered in Mr Crumb's ear. "He wants you."

Mr Crumbs whinnied softly and rested his head on Laura's shoulder.

"Happy Christmas, everyone," said Laura, hugging him. "And a very s pecial Happy Christmas to you, Mr Crumbs – our very own Christmas pony."

Please remember that
ANIMALS ARE FOR LIFE
NOT JUST CHRISTMAS

More books you
might enjoy

The girl who talks to animals

Magic Molly

The Witch's Kitten

HOLLY WEBB

The girl who talks to animals

Magic Molly

The Wish Puppy

HOLLY WEBB

The girl who talks to animals

Magic Molly

The Invisible Bunny

HOLLY WEBB

The girl who talks to animals

Magic Molly

The Shy Piglet

HOLLY WEBB